"I KNEW INSTANTLY THAT I HAD TO HAVE YOU."

He loomed over her like a thunderhead in the darkness. Like lightning his hand flashed toward her, his strong fingers tangling in her hair, snaring her.

Then his mouth was on hers, hungrily. And to her dismay she felt herself responding. Her lips yielded to his eagerly, and her arms, moving under their own power, moved to touch his lean, hard torso.

Inside her head a tiny core of sanity was crying for her to stop . . . to stop before it was too late. . . .

CANDLELIGHT ECSTASY ROMANCES™

SUMMER STORMS

Stephanie St. Clair

A CANDLELIGHT ECSTASY ROMANCE™

Published by
Dell Publishing Co., Inc.
1 Dag Hammarskjold Plaza
New York, New York 10017

Dell ® TM 681510, Dell Publishing Co., Inc.
Candlelight Ecstasy Romance™ is a trademark of
Dell Publishing Co., Inc., New York, New York.

ISBN: 0-440-18444-4

Printed in the United States of America

First printing—February 1982

Dear Reader:

In response to your enthusiasm for Candlelight Ecstasy Romances™, we are now increasing the number of titles per month from three to four.

We are pleased to offer you sensuous novels set in America, depicting modern American women and men as they confront the provocative problems of a modern relationship.

Throughout the history of the Candlelight line, Dell has tried to maintain a high standard of excellence, to give you the finest in reading pleasure. It is now and will remain our most ardent ambition.

Editor
Candlelight Romances

With special thanks to my editors, Vivian Stephens and Ellen Edwards. Thanks also to my agent, Donald Maass, for his many astute suggestions.

CHAPTER 1

It seemed like ages since she had seen the ocean, but it wouldn't be much longer now.

Impatiently cranking the pedals of her reluctant old bicycle, Nicole Tanner looked around anxiously for signs of wind. Here in the center of town there was hardly a rustle from the tall, stately elms.

It was only seven thirty in the morning, of course; the sun was just edging above the gabled rooftops, ready to begin its climb into the cloudless June sky. But a mile away at the shore, she knew, a gentle sea breeze would be starting. It was going to be a perfect day for sailing.

Mannihasset Harbor, Massachusetts, was a charming New England town, but Nicole barely noticed the pretty Victorian houses that lined the shady length of Whitegate Lane. Instead her thoughts fixed on the Howell T. Benton Cup. It was one of the most prestigious prizes a young American sailor could win. Nicole had qualified for the annual competition as a teen-ager and had been bitterly disappointed when a case of summertime flu had prevented her from making the trip to Mannihasset Harbor.

The age limit for the competition was seventeen, and although at twenty-three she was no longer eligible, Nicole was now getting another chance at the Benton Cup just the same. As the summer sailing instructor at the distinguished Watch Point Yacht Club, it would be her responsibility to see that the Cup was successfully defended by a Watch Point sailor, as it had for most of the past sixty years.

The Benton Cup. Suddenly she felt an apprehensive pang in her stomach, but just as quickly willed it away. Worrying about it wouldn't help.

Moving cautiously in the light traffic, she turned right on South Main Street and rode quickly along the broad green past the plain white Congregational Church. Opposite the green were a number of quaint shops. All were closed at this early hour with the exception of the bakery, which was sending the smell of freshly baked bread and cookies into the street.

Anxious to get to the shore, she resisted the temptation to stop. Over a hurried breakfast that morning her new landlady, Emily Petersen, had given her directions. She recited them to herself for the third time: right on South Main, left on Whitaker, right on North Main, left on Harbor Road. Right, left, right, left.

Nicole had never lived far from the sea, and she felt uncomfortable away from it. In the two years since her graduation, her dull entry-level job in the Department of the Interior in Washington had left her with little time for sailing.

Events had taken an unexpected turn just two months ago when she had finally found the career break she was looking for: an offer from a well-known national polling organization in New York. Since it was the perfect opportunity to put her degree in political science to work, she had jumped at it, gratefully quitting her government job before she discovered, to her horror, that her new position wouldn't be open until September.

When a friend from her college sailing team had set her up with this summer job at Watch Point, she had been doubly grateful. Not only would it serve as a stopgap measure, it would also be a welcome interlude before the dreaded move to New York.

Though she wouldn't have admitted it, the vastness of the city depressed her. She had always preferred the friendly scale of the shore, and so she was looking forward to spending the next three months on the water.

New York was far from her thoughts that morning, though, as she pedaled along Whitaker Street, glancing sideways at its Colonial saltbox houses. They were painted a uniform white and stood close to the road behind trim green lawns and low picket fences. Each one had a painted plaque to one side of its door: ABRAHAM CLARK, 1696. JOSHUA WHITAKER, 1672. JERIMIAH BENTON, 1711.

Benton! She started as she saw the name. Could it be that this Jerimiah Benton was an ancestor of Howell T. Benton? Probably, she thought, considering the way New England families tended to stay put. So, the Benton Cup had a pedigree.

Benton. The name was sticking in her head like a top-ten pop tune. Annoyed with herself, Nicole shook her head and turned right, following North Main Street away from the center of town.

She had gone almost half a mile before she realized that she had missed the turnoff to Harbor Road. Scolding herself, she quickly turned around and started back the way she had come. Just ahead was a small gas station, and she decided to ask directions rather than miss the turn again. Her bike rattled and clanked as she rode over a small bump and braked to a halt in front of the station door.

Hearing her pull up, a young man in overalls ambled out and said in a friendly tone, "Fill a up?" His New England twang sounded strange to Nicole, but not unpleasant.

Laughing, she replied, "No, the tank's full, thanks. Can you just direct me to Harbor Road?"

"Sure thing," the boy replied, pointing down the road. "About three hundred yards along you'll see the Center Pharmacy on your right. The corner's right there. You can't miss it."

"Thanks," Nicole said with a smile, pushing off and coasting down to the street. She hadn't gone twenty yards when she heard a playful whistle from behind her.

Turning, she saw that a second attendant had joined the first in the door of the station. The two of them gave her a friendly wave, and she flushed with embarrassment. Those brats!

Though she was fairly old-fashioned in most things, Nicole hated glib displays of male superiority—one of the characteristics that had helped her earn a reputation as a deadly sailor. For a moment she considered sending a stinging remark back at the young men, but decided against it. Instead she flashed them a saucy smile that said "Don't you wish . . . !" and continued on her way. That would fix them!

Nicole had never thought of herself as particularly attractive, though she often received compliments on her looks. Her finely drawn face—with its straight nose, pouting lips, and smoky gray eyes—was both sensual and innocent, and never failed to draw second glances. Her wispy, light brown hair was attractively clipped and parted on one side of her head with boyish charm, leaving the delicate lines of her face uncluttered. She was fairly short, but her petite figure curved gently in all the right places. Riding along in her close-fitting jeans, bright yellow T-shirt, and open-toed sandals, she was quite a pretty sight—though she wouldn't have believed it.

She found Harbor Road without further trouble and turned the corner, determined to enjoy the scenery. The white wooden houses on either side were modern and larger than those in the center of town. Sitting on wide landscaped lawns, they were elegant, yet none of them was in the least ostentatious. The residents of Mannihasset Harbor were obviously more anxious to preserve the New England charm of their town than to display their wealth. Nothing like good old Yankee self-assurance, she thought.

Presently she found herself riding through a pleasant stretch of humid green woods. The stately elms of the town had given way to white-barked birch trees, leafy maples, and clusters of pine. The ground was thick with new summer growth. Caseweed and mulberry bushes were everywhere, and the sassafras trees perfumed the cool morning air.

Finally the woods ended and the open, marshy ground with its high cattails told her that she was nearing the ocean. Her pulse quickened as she heard the lonely barking of sea gulls and tasted the familiar salt tang in the air. The road climbed a small hill, and at the top was a stunning view of the harbor. Nicole stopped to look across an expanse of calm blue water to the low peninsula that formed the harbor, curving around like a forefinger circling to meet the thumb of the mainland.

Mannihæsset had never been large or deep enough for commercial shipping, but it was a perfectly protected haven for pleasure boats. Indeed, it had been a popular summer resort for wealthy Bostonians for more than a hundred years. Since there were few natural beaches along this stretch of the coast, the chief summer sport here was sailing. And the standard and focal point of sailing in this part of the world had always been, without dispute, the Watch Point Yacht Club.

At the head of the harbor, perhaps a half mile away, was the yacht club itself, sitting squarely on its own granite island. Even at this distance she was impressed with its extravagance: it was a monument to nineteenth-century industry and opulence.

An exceptionally tall flagpole, crossed by a yardarm two thirds of the way up, stood in front of the building with the club's triangular burgee stirring gently at its top. Beyond that, through the harbor's narrow mouth, Nicole could see a tiny bit of the Atlantic Ocean, the cloudless blue sky coming down to meet it in the straight, unbroken line of the horizon.

Nicole stood by the side of the road with a wistful smile on her face. *It's like coming home,* she thought. Reflected in the still water of the harbor, the yacht club had a timelessness to it that captivated her. This was going to be a special summer.

With a curious mixture of anxiety and relief she climbed on her bike and coasted down the hill, following the road to the edge of the water. Soon she was gliding beneath the high arching branches of the massive trees on Oak Lane, which ran up the length of the peninsula to the club.

Hidden behind moss-covered stone walls, high green hedges, and wrought-iron gates were some of the most beautiful homes she had ever seen. With their lawns sweeping down to the water, they were like miniature estates. Built for the leisurely summers of an era gone by, the lower floors were surrounded by broad porches, and

14

Nicole half expected to see maids in starched caps and stiff white aprons setting tables for morning tea.

Idly she wondered if she would ever be able to afford such a graceful way of life. Probably not, she decided. One had to be born to this kind of wealth.

Oak Lane ended in a small circle with a tiny bandstand in its center. On the far side was a small parking area, and as she brought her bike to a stop she saw two stone posts marking the entrance to a walkway. A weathered bronze plaque was fixed to the post on the right. It read: WATCH POINT YACHT CLUB. MEMBERS ONLY.

Oh, yeah? she thought, grinning to herself as she pushed the bike to one side to park it. After lacing the security chain through the spokes and frame, she snapped the lock shut with a loud click, tucked her hands into the back pockets of her jeans, and stolled jauntily through the stone gate and down a cement path to the water's edge. There a wooden bridge ran across a narrow channel of water, zigzagging between several large boulders, ending at the steps of the yacht club itself.

Nicole held her breath involuntarily for a moment. Up close the building was even more magnificent. She wouldn't be able to get inside this early in the morning, of course, but she had come so far, it seemed a shame not to have a closer look. She jogged across the footbridge, hearing waves rippling below her, and bounded up the final half-dozen steps to the broad covered porch that surrounded the club on all four sides.

In the early morning quiet Nicole had the eerie feeling that hidden eyes were watching her as she crossed to a pair of mahogany double doors. Nervously glancing over her shoulder, she absently pulled on a large brass handle and was surprised to feel the door swing outward.

It was unlocked! She would be able to explore inside

after all. Pulling harder, she managed to open the heavy door just enough for her to slip her trim body inside.

She found herself in a wide wood-floored entrance hall, which smelled pleasantly of varnish and newly circulated sea air. She paused, listening for the sound of people moving about elsewhere in the building. Hearing nothing, she called out, "Hello! Anybody here?"

There was no reply except for the loud tick of a clock in another room.

Feeling a bit like Alice in Wonderland, she looked around her. A broad carpeted stairway rose to the second-floor hallway, and on either side of her was an equally inviting doorway. Farther down the hall she noticed a large glass-fronted cabinet, and she stepped softly across the creaky wooden floor to have a look.

Inside was a collection of gleaming silver trophies and polished wood plaques. Sitting proudly in the place of honor was an ornate two-and-a-half-foot-high cup. Nicole felt her heart thumping heavily as she leaned over to read the inscription etched on the face of its bowl: HOWELL T. BENTON CUP.

So, this was the trophy she was charged with defending this summer. Seeing the Cup itself for the first time somehow made the challenge seem very real. Nicole felt a knot forming in her stomach again. What if Watch Point lost the cup this summer? A long tradition of championship sailing was in her hands.

She brushed aside her fears after a moment. The trophy was only a symbol, after all. Her real challenge would be out on the water, teaching her young students to sail like champions. She was a champion herself, and if she couldn't do it, who could?

Still, the cup had been sitting in its place at Watch Point for longer than she had been alive. She couldn't help

16

feeling slightly intimidated as she bent over to examine the rows of tiny brass plates set into the trophy's pedestal. Starting with the year 1921, they listed the winners of the Cup and their respective yacht clubs—nearly always Watch Point.

Looking closer, she saw that one young sailor had won the Cup six years running. What a record! He would have been twelve, at the oldest, the first time he won. The plates were slightly tarnished and she had to peer closely to make out the name, but after a moment she did. James E. Benton.

Another Benton! A family of overachievers, certainly.

James E. Benton. The name caused her to pull her brows together. She knew that name, she was sure. He was famous, wasn't he?

Suddenly she snapped her fingers and stood up. Of course! James Benton: twice an Olympic gold medalist for the U.S.A. and now the terror of the exclusive ocean racing circuit, his name was practically synonymous with winning.

For some reason she couldn't understand, Nicole felt a chill run through her. James Benton was a highly respected, if controversial, figure in the world of sailboat racing. Now she would be responsible for the defense of a trophy he had won six times—a trophy that bore his family name.

Would he take a personal interest in the competition or not? His impressive string of wins had ended nearly fifteen years ago. Did he even remember them? He probably hadn't even been back to Watch Point for many years.

Yet something told her that this was not so. His family's history was obviously closely tied to Mannihasset Harbor. Perhaps he still lived here year round.

"Can I help you?" came a voice quite suddenly from behind her.

Startled, she whirled around and saw a tall sandy-haired young man leaning comfortably against the stairway banister with his hands tucked in his pockets. He was about her own age, dressed in deck shoes, tan slacks, and work shirt, with the sleeves rolled up to the elbows. Even as she stared at him in surprise she couldn't help but notice his bright blue eyes and pleasant, tanned face, which at the moment was wearing a quizzical expression.

"No, I . . . that is, I was only just—" she stammered, taken aback by his sudden appearance. How had he managed to sneak up behind her on the creaky wooden floor without being heard? Had she been that engrossed in her thoughts?

"I hope you weren't thinking of taking that home with you," he said, referring to the Benton Cup.

"No, of course not. I already have an ashtray," she replied, beginning to get her bearings.

"Good, you'd find it pretty difficult to lift anyway. It's bolted down," the young man replied with mock-relief. "My name's Steve Fulton, by the way. I'm the dockmaster here."

"Nicole Tanner," she returned, holding out her hand. Without giving the matter a second thought, she decided she liked him.

"Pleased to meet you," he said seriously, taking her hand in a firm grasp. "Are you a new member?"

"Well, no, not exactly. I thought I'd take a look around the club, if that's okay. I'm the new sailing instructor."

To her surprise Steve looked startled at this announcement. From his expression she might have told him she was from Mars.

His expression quickly returned to a grin, however. "Glad to have you aboard. The building's generally unlocked while I'm here, which is most of the time, so you can come mess around whenever you like. If you ever need anything, just give a shout."

Why had he looked at her so strangely when she told him who she was? Questions were spinning around in her head, but she let them go for the time being.

"Thanks," she said aloud, "but where will I find you?"

"Down at the gas dock generally. It's just below the porch on the other side of the building."

Nicole still looked disoriented. Seeing this, Steve offered, "Look, why don't I give you the grand tour of this joint? There's no one around right now. When we're through, you can come down and help me knock off a cup of coffee."

"Great!" she answered with genuine enthusiasm. She was still faintly troubled by his odd look a moment before, but she had the feeling she would need a friend that summer, and she eagerly followed as he led her through the doorway at the end of the hall, pointing out old photographs of Watch Point as they went.

"Here you go." Steve handed her a steaming mug of freshly brewed coffee.

Nicole accepted it with a smile of thanks, but the sides of the mug were hotter than she had expected. She set it down hastily on the top of his ancient wooden desk, spilling some of the coffee in the process.

"I'm sorry. What a klutz I'm being," she apologized.

"My fault. Don't worry about it," Steve said diplomatically. "That old desk has soaked up everything from ketchup to crankcase oil. I don't think a little coffee will hurt it any."

As he mopped up the spill with a rag, Nicole glanced around at his tidy workbench and the rows of tools hung

19

neatly on the pegboard walls. Steve appeared to be anything but sloppy.

"In fact," he continued, "you're welcome to come spill coffee with me anytime. The club is so dedicated to spit 'n' polish that it's nice to have a place where I can relax and make a mess if I want to."

Nicole laughed and nodded her head in agreement. The club was indeed spotless, from the gleaming mahogany paneling in the grand ballroom to the shiny brass doorknob of the cubbyhole on the third floor that would be her office. What had impressed her most, though, was the nautical paraphernalia scattered everywhere. Antique maps of the New England coast hung on the walls and ships' wheels of every size decorated the second-floor hallway. Watch Point was steeped in tradition, and apparently proud of the fact.

Even Steve was infected with the club's heritage. As he walked her through the building he had run through a surprising repertoire of anecdotes and historical facts, though he also had an amusing list of complaints about some of the stuffier members and their grim preoccupation with rules and regulations. His running commentary had kept her laughing all the way to his office, where they now sat. Static from a VHF radio by her elbow crackled quietly under their conversation.

"Most of the members are quite wealthy, as you can imagine," he was saying, his feet braced on an open drawer. "They pay a small fortune in annual dues, so they expect excellent service from the club's employees. That's perfectly okay by me, but some of them also seem to feel that we're their personal servants—like chauffeurs or butlers."

Nicole frowned. "I think I would find that pretty hard

to take." In fact there was hardly anything she hated more than condescension.

"I don't think you need to worry too much," Steve reassured her. "You'll find yourself in a different category than, say, me or the waitresses in the dining room. Everyone's concerned about keeping Watch Point on top in junior competition. Especially Benton."

Benton! That name again. Suddenly Nicole felt her throat going dry, though she couldn't think why it should.

"Um . . . do you mean *James* Benton?" she managed to croak.

For the second time that morning Steve gave her an odd look. "Of course, who else?" he said, seemingly surprised that she should have to ask at all.

So, James Benton *was* a member of Watch Point. The news set her mind racing. Meeting such a living legend would be frightening, but would also be a rare opportunity to pick up some pointers. She had to know more about the man.

Trying to appear casual, she leaned back and asked, "But why would he be concerned with the junior sailing classes? Does he have children in the program?"

Steve laughed. "Children! The Playboy of the Western World? He's not even married, let alone a parent. No, didn't you know? He's the commodore of the club."

Nicole slumped down in her chair, stunned. Commodore! James Benton was her boss? Well, obviously. As the club's elected president he would be in charge of every aspect of its operation. The thought made her heart sink. The man's passion for technical perfection and his fanatical devotion to winning were notorious. How could she possibly hope to meet his standards?

"Oh," she said weakly, "I didn't know. Does he really take that much interest in my job?"

21

Steve raised his eyebrows. "You'd better believe it! Most of the time it seems that's the *only* thing he takes an interest in around here. He's supposed to be head honcho, but in reality he delegates most of his responsibilities to the club's manager and various committees." He paused to sip his coffee.

Nicole pondered this information. There seemed to be no doubt about it: she was going to have to deal with the man.

"So you think I'll actually get to meet him?" she asked, needing to have the fact confirmed.

"*Meet* him!" Steve exclaimed. "I'd say a head-on collision would be more likely, if past experience is anything to go by. He's quite a tyrant."

Her head was spinning. Nervously she set her mug on the desk. This was certainly more than she had bargained for. The last thing she wanted was to spend her last whole summer by the sea locking horns with an arrogant prima donna.

"I'm surprised you didn't know all this before," Steve commented. "Didn't Benton interview you for the job?"

"No, I've never met him, or anyone from the club for that matter," she explained. "I was a substitution for someone on the sailing team at school who originally had the job. He had to give it up at the last moment when he got a berth on a research schooner. He recommended me. I've won some important races, so I guess the Junior Sailing Committee figured I'd be as good as anybody."

"That would explain it. Benton's been in the Middle East on business for the last month, I'm told. I wonder if he even knows you've been hired yet."

Nicole had to admit that he might not, which would make matters worse. Would he force the committee to

22

replace her with someone he had personally approved? She twisted uneasily in her chair.

Seeing her distress, Steve added hastily, "Oh, there's nothing he can do about it really. The committee officially does the hiring. Besides, classes start in another week and I can't imagine that he'd want to try to find someone else on such short notice. You shouldn't have anything to worry about."

"Shouldn't?"

"Well, it's just that—" Steve hesitated, brushing back his sandy hair with his fingers.

"Just what?" she pressed. Better to know the worst now.

Steve's discomfort was obvious. "It's just that in the four years I've been working here, you're the first female I've seen in this job."

"What!" Nicole was incredulous. So, that was why he had given her the odd look earlier. She felt herself growing angry. "*That* shouldn't make a bit of difference to anybody, least of all James Benton! He can't hold my sex against me. There are laws about discriminating on the basis of—"

"Whoa! Don't get me wrong," Steve put in, holding up his palms. "I don't mean that you're going to be a victim of discrimination, only that he's going to be a little surprised."

Tough luck for him, she thought to herself. She was as good a sailor as any man her own age. Better than most, in fact. "Just wait until he starts pushing me around," she said hotly. "He'll find out quickly that he's got some adjustments to make."

"No doubt. He's used to different methods of persuasion with women, I think," Steve said dryly.

"Ha! He'd better not try any funny business, either—"

23

"I don't think you need to worry on that score," Steve cut in. "From what I've seen I wouldn't say you're his type."

Thank goodness for that, she told herself automatically. Yet something about Steve's remark troubled her. Distantly she was aware of a sense of disappointment, but she quickly smothered it.

"In any case it's not as bad as it seems," Steve went on. "Most of the time he's away on business. Or else he's off racing that boat of his."

Her ears perked up. "You mean *Warlord?*" she asked.

He nodded. Nicole had seen pictures of Benton's state-of-the-art yacht on the covers of more than one sailing magazine. With its vicious-looking pitch-black hull it had looked super-fast.

Although she was used to sailing on small one-design boats, she had crewed on large custom-made ocean racers a few times. These sleek "racing machines," as they were called, were awesome to behold. Flying across the ocean with every possible square foot of sail aloft was a heady sensation. It would be exciting to get a close-up look at *Warlord,* even if it did belong to James Benton.

"Does he keep it moored here?"

"No, it was here once last summer, but only for a few days." Steve looked at his watch and placed his feet on the floor. "Speaking of boats, let me show you the dinghies you'll be using for the classes. One of the sailing instructor's chores is to rig them for the summer, and I'm sure you'll want to get going as soon as you can."

Instantly her mind was back to business. There would be a great deal to do: schedules, lesson plans, and of course an inventory of the equipment. "Terrific. Lead the way," she said.

Steve sprang out of his chair and led her out the door.

His office was actually a small hut at one end of the gas dock, which floated below the porch on the harbor side of the club. Hurrying to keep up with his lanky strides, she followed him up a dolly ramp and around the porch to the back side of the building. There Steve stopped, flipped through his fat ring of keys, and unlocked a pair of wide wooden doors.

A few concrete steps led down to a musty-smelling cellar. Steve switched on a bare overhead bulb and Nicole looked around her.

Propped against the walls were a dozen dinghy hulls. They had been painted white at one time, but after a winter in the damp cellar all but a few were blistered and flaking.

She groaned. Each of the hulls would have to be scraped, sanded, and repainted before the boats could be rigged and put in the water. That was several days worth of work, at least! Suddenly weary, she flopped down on the cellar steps and cupped her chin in her hand. She should have known this job wouldn't be a joyride. First James Benton, and now this.

Steve sat down next to her. "Problems?"

"Not really. I was just thinking about all the work those hulls are going to need."

Steve tore a sheet of paper from the clipboard he was carrying and handed her a pen from his shirt pocket. "Make a list of all the things you'll need right away and then take a ride down to Bensen's Marine in town. I'll give you a hand with the work; I have some electric sanders and paint sprayers that should make things easier."

Nicole brightened. "Thanks, but how will I get the supplies in from town? I only have a bicycle, and that's on its last legs."

"They'll deliver. Just be sure to get a receipt so I can

25

verify the delivery against your purchase order. Charge it to the club's account."

She nodded. "Roger."

"I'll leave you to it, then. I've got some other stuff to take care of." He started up the steps, but paused at the top. Looking a bit embarrassed, he asked, "By the way, you know the Opening Ball is tomorrow night?"

"No, I didn't. Am I invited?"

"Actually, I think you *have* to be there. It's customary for the commodore to introduce the staff to the membership."

Nicole felt a tremor of anxiety run through her. So, there would be no putting off her encounter with the notorious Benton. Couldn't she be left in peace for a few days?

"Anyway, if you have no one to go with, I'd be happy to bring you myself," Steve went on, slightly red in the face.

Immediately Nicole felt her tension ease. The evening would certainly be easier with Steve there to give her moral support.

Giving him an encouraging smile, she said, "Terrific! I'd like that."

Steve looked relieved. "Okay, see you later, then." With a wave he was gone.

It didn't take long for her to draw up a list of supplies. In half an hour she was locking the cellar door behind her and trotting back across the footbridge and up the path to her bicycle. A moment later she was pedaling back down Oak Lane, retracing her steps back to town.

Despite her resolve to keep her mind fixed on the business at hand, the news about James Benton crept back into her thoughts. Steve's description fit all she had read about him. He was a champion to be sure, but success had evidently not made a gentleman out of him. On the contrary, his aggressive pursuit of glory had made him quite a few enemies in the world of ocean racing.

She had met his type before—loud, overbearing, and arrogant. He was probably a fat cigar-smoker too! If what Steve had said was true, he would be determined to make trouble for her. It simply wasn't right that someone could judge her before she had a chance to prove herself! The thought made her grit her teeth angrily.

She reached the rise that overlooked the harbor and paused again. The bright blue sky was now punctuated by fluffy white cumulus clouds. A breeze gently rustled her short hair, and she could see clusters of dark ripples chasing each other across the surface of the water. She had been right: it was indeed going to be a perfect day for sailing.

Nicole resolved to put her uneasiness away. Besides, it was silly to anticipate the worst from someone she hadn't yet met. For all she knew, all that she had read about Benton in magazines was merely journalistic exaggeration. Briefly it occurred to her that Steve had not seemed the type to exaggerate, but she pushed the thought out of her head. It was too nice a day for fruitless worrying.

Pushing off, she coasted down the hill and on through the marshy stretch of lowland, finally reaching the woods that led to town. The pleasant, earthy smell of thick vegetation was in her nostrils. She noticed bunches of wild violets by the roadside, and here and there she could see the thorny tendrils of wild raspberry bushes.

Raspberries! It had been ages since she had tasted them. She decided to stop and sample the wares at the next opportunity.

She saw her chance not a minute later. Near the beginning of a sharp bend in the road, on the opposite side, was a large bush loaded with the red fruit. She brought her bike to a halt on the sandy shoulder, pushing the kickstand down with her foot. The bike teetered for a moment but caught its balance and stood still. Leaving it, she started eagerly across the road.

She was no more than a step or two into the street when she suddenly became aware of the high-speed whine of an approaching car. She would have to hurry.

It was already very close. In the periphery of her vision she caught the sudden flash of sunlight reflected off a windshield as it shot around the bend.

It was too late to turn back. Immediately her reflexes took over and she threw herself the rest of the way across the road. A horn blared as she fell heavily into the thorny undergrowth.

A sickening squeal of tires shattered the air, followed a split second later by a loud crash. The car had missed her by inches!

Her heart was beating wildly and her breath came in short, sudden gasps. Feeling nauseated, Nicole slumped facedown on the ground and shut her eyes. She felt as if she were going to pass out.

She was unsure whether only seconds or several minutes had passed when she heard the slam of a car door and the sound of low swearing.

She tried to raise herself on one elbow but felt a strong hand on her shoulder holding her down. An angry voice in her ear commanded, "Lie still. Don't move."

The unexpected authority of that order pinned her to the ground far more effectively than the weight on her shoulder. After a long moment she drew in a breath and said, "I think I'm okay, thank you," but she was alarmed to hear the tremor in her voice.

28

"Don't move until you're sure you're all right. Tell me if it hurts anywhere." The voice was deep and masculine, but despite the concern the words expressed she could hear the controlled anger behind them.

"No, I'm not hurt. Just a little bruised."

The pressure on her shoulder relaxed, and she pushed herself up and on to her side. The world was spinning slightly, but at the still center of her vision floated a face that was shockingly handsome. In an instant she took in the rugged cut of its features, well-tanned skin, and a shock of unruly black hair.

But what held her spellbound were the man's eyes. They were a fierce, steely blue-gray—the color of the ocean on an angry winter afternoon. She was utterly unable to look away from him. It was as if some powerful magnetic force hidden in his eyes were preventing her from turning her head.

For an unbearably long minute his eyes probed her. His hard face was expressionless, but she could sense a piercing intelligence at work behind it. What could he be looking for in her eyes? She flushed uncomfortably but could only return his look helplessly. She wanted to speak but could find no words to bring to her lips.

Gradually, though, he shifted his weight away from her. She watched, transfixed, as his features relaxed almost imperceptibly. He lifted his chin slightly, and the movement magically seemed to break his spell over her.

He rose to an impressive height and asked, "You can get up now."

The tone of command in those words irritated her, but nevertheless she slowly stood up, dusting herself off as she did. Her bright yellow T-shirt was streaked with dirt and her bare arms were covered with scratches.

By contrast the tall figure next to her was fresh and tidy,

unruffled by the near accident. He was dressed in an impeccably cut three-piece suit, a dark silk tie, and a pin-striped shirt with a gold stick pin through the collar. Could this be the same person who had come ripping down the road like a teen-age hot-rodder?

On second glance his wild good looks seemed incongruous with his clothes. Quite unasked for came the thought that he would look more natural wearing no clothes at all.

Quickly suppressing the image, Nicole glanced down the road. Sitting sideways in the middle of the street about ten yards away was a gleaming gray Mercedes. Long black tire marks stretched backward up the surface of the road to where they stood.

No, there was no doubt about it. This was the driver of the car that had almost hit her.

Still shaky, Nicole looked around for her bicycle. It was not standing where she had left it. Keenly aware of the stranger's eyes following her, she walked unsteadily down the road, stopping suddenly.

The bike was lying in a patch of tall weeds, crushed and bent wildly out of shape. As it skidded sideways the unscratched Mercedes had knocked the bike off the road as easily as a tennis player returning a volley.

Dumbfoundedly she looked at the twisted mass of useless metal. Her head was getting light. A second later and it would have been she lying by the roadside, broken and bleeding. She began to weave on her feet.

Instantly she felt two strong hands grip her arms from behind. His taut, resonant voice said quietly in her ear, "Steady. It's over now."

Suddenly she was angry. She whirled around dangerously, breaking his grip, and spat, "I'm perfectly all right, thank you!"

But as she said it she knew she was not.

30

The world fizzled into blackness and she felt herself falling backward. Two strong arms circled her quickly and then she was being held tightly against a broad, hard chest. She slumped against him, letting him support her entirely.

All at once the boundaries of the world were reduced to the arms that were holding her so securely. Nicole felt herself sinking into their safe, strong circle as if she had always belonged there. A warm, satisfied glow began somewhere deep within her. She could hear the distant *thump-thump* of a heart at work.

Some time later she raised her head to look at the face above her with a soft, puzzled expression. The dark eyes that looked down at her were full of tenderness. Funny, hadn't he been angry a minute ago? Or was it an hour ago?

Before she had time to figure this out, he bent his head to kiss her.

Suddenly her mind snapped awake. This was the man who had nearly killed her!

With a cry of surprise she wriggled from his embrace and stepped backward, wide awake and alert. She saw a look of surprise on his face fade, quickly turning instead to a twisted grin.

The colossal nerve of the man! Taking advantage of her moment of dizziness had been inexcusable. She waited for him to say something, but he did not speak. His eyes burned at her as if she were the one who ought to be apologizing.

To her chagrin that was just what she found herself doing. "I—I'm sorry. I didn't mean to—" she stammered, hoping to fill the void of silence between them, but hating the words coming out of her mouth.

Immediately he seized on her mistake. "That's quite all

31

right. You were about to faint; perfectly understandable under the circumstances."

She thought she detected an objectionable double meaning to his words, but she couldn't be sure. "Maybe," she said, "but I'm usually not so easily shaken."

"Did I shake you so badly?" he returned, his eyes gleaming with cruel amusement. Now what did he mean? He was twisting her words to humiliate her.

Testily she shot back, "No, of course not. I'm just not used to being run down on quiet roads, that's all."

Instantly he raised himself to his full height, which was substantial, and gave her a look that would have withered a samurai swordsman. Nicole fought to keep from cringing. The aura of power surrounding him was almost tangible.

His voice cold with icy disapproval, he said, "No, of course not. But then again I didn't actually run you down."

Nicole burned. Was he going to deny that he had almost killed her? This was too much. He had been driving like a maniac.

"Well, you very nearly did. If I hadn't jumped out of the way, I might be looking like raw hamburger meat right now."

"Jumped *out* of the way? It looked more like you stepped *into* the way to me."

Nicole's mouth flew open in amazement. Was he suggesting that she had deliberately stepped out in front of his speeding car? That would be suicide!

In spite of his intimidating air, her anger rose. "Well, I don't come from around here, but in most states pedestrians have the right of way."

Oddly he seemed to enjoy her challenge. Casually he put his hands in his trouser pockets and said in an unexpectedly easy voice, "Certainly. But most pedestrians also have some common sense. They generally look both ways before crossing the street."

His ironic tone made her blood boil. *I'll give him a taste of his own medicine,* she thought. "Of course I look where I'm going! I walk in front of speeding cars all the time. Some of them even slow down."

"Yes, I'm afraid I did manage to avoid you," he answered with crushing sarcasm. "Try a little harder next time and you might actually succeed in getting yourself killed."

"Don't worry," she replied in a frosty voice. "There won't be a next time, you can be sure."

"Oh?" he queried. There was a harshness in his voice that suggested that he didn't intend to let the issue rest there. He seemed about to pursue it further, but after a moment he changed his mind and said simply, "We'll see. Now get in the car."

"What!"

"I said get in the car. Or do you intend to walk from here to wherever you're going?"

Was he out of his mind? First he had nearly run her over with his car, and now he wanted her to get *into* it and let him drive her? Not in a million years!

"I'm perfectly capable of taking care of myself, thank you," she said stiffly.

"Yes, we just had an admirable demonstration of that fact. However, it's more than a mile to the center of town and half a mile back to the beach, if that's where you're headed. Considering the shock you've had, I don't think you want to risk the possibility of heat exhaustion, don't you agree? Good. Now get in the car."

How insufferably arrogant the man was! She didn't intend to ride in his car for one yard, let alone all the way back to the center of town.

"I'll look after myself, thank you," she declared.

"Don't be a fool," he said in a dangerous tone. "Please don't argue any further."

With that he walked past her and opened the passenger door of the Mercedes. She could see that trying to reason with him would do no good. Angrily she followed him to the car, flung herself into the front seat, and pulled the door closed with a slam.

She sat tensely, looking straight ahead with her arms folded. Behind her she could hear him unlocking the trunk and placing her ruined bicycle in. A moment later came the muffled thump of the lid closing. She hoped he would find something else to detain him, but a second later he was opening the door on the driver's side and climbing in next to her. She squeezed herself as close to her own door as she could.

Without a word he started the car, executed a neat three-point turn, and started off down the road, driving with surprising care. Nicole was fuming. She had no intention of speaking to the man, but after a minute he turned to her and said, "Do you propose to tell me where we're going?"

She gave him the Petersens' address in a clipped monotone, still staring straight ahead of her. He turned back to his driving, saying nothing more.

As they drove, the uneasy silence was broken only by the quiet hum of the tires on the road and the low whistle of wind rushing past her open window. The sudden burst of fear she had felt at the time of the accident had vanished completely, but she was still in turmoil. In a few brief minutes he had put her through as great a range of emotion as she had experienced in her entire life.

She found herself wanting to look sideways and study him. She stopped herself, though. No doubt he would catch her in the act and humiliate her with another one of his stinging remarks.

Still silent, they drove through a double row of tall elm trees that arched gracefully overhead, forming a cool green tunnel over the road. As the trees flicked past her window one by one, she saw each one of them standing in sharp relief to its background. With the sun shining from above, their leaves were a more vivid green than she could ever remember seeing before.

She discovered that the whole day, in fact, had come into sharp focus. It was as if a filmy gauze had been lifted from her eyes for the first time in twenty-three years. Every tiny sound that reached her ears seemed as crisp and distinct as the crack of a rifle.

Nicole blinked her eyes. What was causing this state of heightened perception? Had the man drugged her somehow? Perhaps she was only just becoming aware of her new surroundings. Yes, that must be it. In a few days the novelty of Mannihasset Harbor would begin to wear off, and as everything fell into a state of comfortable familiarity, the man next to her would be just another careless driver.

Deep down, though, she wasn't sure this was true. She was curious about him in spite of herself. She decided to question him, but as she turned to speak she saw that they were turning into the Petersens' driveway.

The car came to a stop, and without a word he went around to open the trunk. Nicole climbed out, and as she saw him lifting her crumpled bicycle out, she realized for the first time that now she was without any means of transportation. As he leaned the twisted form against the side of the house, she gave an involuntary cry of frustration.

Wheeling around at the sound, he said with a trace of sarcasm, "Don't tell me you're only beginning to feel the effects now? Don't worry, you're perfectly all right. A little rest will solve all your problems."

Nicole flinched as his eyes burned into hers. "No, it's not that. It's just that my bike is useless now. I have no way of getting around anymore."

He regarded her silently for a minute, as if he were sizing her up. *Probably wondering whether I'll sue him,* she thought. She hoped that he would at least offer to pay for a replacement.

It was then that she noticed his eyes traveling up and down her figure, measuring her with a frankness that took her breath away altogether. She felt naked under his gaze. Even though the morning air had grown quite hot, she shuddered. The nerve of the man! She formed a cutting remark, but it stuck in her throat.

For a moment she was utterly paralyzed. She was sure she knew what was on his mind, but when he finally spoke, he was referring to her bike.

"It looks like you'll have to get a new one," he said simply, and without another word he walked over to his car with a few long strides, hopped in, and backed it out of the driveway.

With a roar he was gone, leaving only a faint cloud of exhaust in the road.

CHAPTER 2

Nicole burned with rage. How completely inconsiderate of him! Yet how predictable that he should drive off without offering compensation for her wrecked bicycle. It wasn't as if he couldn't afford to, either. If his clothes and car were any indication of his financial status, he could easily have bought her twenty bicycles.

Clenching her fists, she fought to control her temper. No one with that much money could truly be so miserly. She would simply telephone him and ask him for the money. Confronted with his penury, he would probably feel guilty and relent.

With a start she realized that she hadn't asked his name. She hadn't even bothered to look at the number of his license plate. How stupid she had been!

"Who was that?" Emily Petersen asked, coming out of the kitchen door. She was a round, white-haired woman with a kind, grandmotherly face of the sort that Nicole had thought didn't exist in real life. Glad to hear her friendly voice, Nicole replied, "I don't know. But whoever he is, I don't like him."

She proceeded to describe the accident to Emily, leaving out the details of the minutes she had spent in the man's arms.

Emily listened sympathetically, gasping when she saw the ruined hulk that had been the bicycle. "Well, that certainly does beat all," she remarked. "How impossibly rude!"

"The worst part is, I have no way to get around now, and there are tons of things I have to do," Nicole lamented.

Emily's expression was thoughtful. "You know, I think we might be able to help you out. As I recall we still have our daughter Pamela's old bike in the back of the garage. She left it here when she moved out to California to get married."

Leading her over to the detached garage at the end of the driveway, Emily folded back its old-fashioned doors. She rummaged around in the darkness for a minute, then wheeled out an old, rusty-looking bicycle. Nicole examined it in dismay: it was in worse shape than hers had been. A worn-out wicker basket hung from its handlebars and the chain was missing.

"It needs some cleaning up, but I'll put my husband to work on it. He's the mechanical genius around here," Emily said.

Not wishing to appear ungrateful, Nicole answered, "Thank you. I would like to borrow it, if I may." Indeed, she had no other choice.

"For heaven's sake, I'm sure you can just keep it. Pam doesn't need it anymore and it's just rusting to pieces back there. Now, come along inside. You look like you could use some lunch."

38

Obediently Nicole followed her indoors. The mysterious Mercedes driver had certainly managed to make her life complicated in a very short space of time. A new bike was out of the question. Her salary at Watch Point was far from generous, and she would need to save as much as she could if she were to have enough to get started in New York in September.

What a selfish baboon! *How could I have thought him attractive, even for a minute?* she wondered as she sat down to the sandwich that Emily had put on the kitchen table for her. She wondered how he made his living; dishonestly, no doubt.

She finished the sandwich and a glass of lemonade in record time. With food in her stomach her anger diminished somewhat and she began to feel drowsy. After washing her plate and glass, she climbed up to her attic room and flopped down on the soft quilt-covered bed.

A cool, pine-scented breeze drifted between the windows at either end of the room. As she closed her eyes and relaxed, the tension and anger she had felt earlier evaporated. Her thoughts wandered and she remembered the warm, comfortable sensation of being held in the man's arms.

A sudden, lonely ache came over her and she shook the memory from her head. She would never see him again, which was probably just as well. No matter how good-looking, he was still a creep. Besides, she had too many other things to think about.

Mentally she began to review her new responsibilities, but fatigue caught up with her and after a few minutes she had fallen into a light sleep.

"Nicole!"

Nicole's eyes shot open, but her mind was still cloudy.

Groggily she lifted her head from her pillow, getting her bearings. Dusty yellow light slanted in from the back window, making a long rectangle on the floor. It was late afternoon. She had been asleep for several hours, she realized.

"Nicole!" Emily's slightly agitated voice drifted up the stairs once again.

"Coming!" she called out, springing up from the bed. Snatching her hairbrush from its place on the bureau, she quickly put her rumpled hair back into order, then shot through her door and down two flights of stairs to the front hall.

Emily was standing by the front door with a perplexed look on her face. "Oh, Nicole dear! I'm sorry to disturb you, but there's a boy here who has a package for you. You hadn't mentioned that you were expecting anything, so I thought I'd better call you down."

"Package?" she echoed dumbly. What package? She had brought all her gear for the summer with her the day before on the train to Boston.

On the front porch, shifting impatiently from one foot to another, was a young man in overalls. Next to him was a large cardboard box. "Will you sign for this please?" he asked quickly, holding out a clipboard and pen.

"Wait, sign for what?" she asked, mystified.

"Peugeot," the boy answered simply.

Peugeot? A foreign car? No, it couldn't be. Not in such a small box. She was more mystified than ever.

Then suddenly she understood. "You mean it's a bicycle? I didn't order this," she declared, knowing perfectly well who had.

"No," the boy said. "A guy came into the store and said to deliver this to the young lady at this address. I guess that's you. If you want, I'll put it together for you."

Dumbfoundedly Nicole searched for a reply. Taking her silence as an answer in the affirmative, the boy quickly opened the box and began pulling out an assortment of parts.

Helplessly Nicole looked toward Emily. "It looks like we were wrong about that young man," she said, smiling.

Nicole disagreed but bit her lip to keep from saying so. Stopping only to run to his van for tools, the boy had the bike together in a matter of minutes. After spraying the gears and chain with silicone oil, he stood up, wiped his hands on his overalls, and said, "There you go. Try it out."

She examined the bike appreciatively. It had a light-weight aluminum frame, a ten-speed gearbox, and handlebars that curved downward. Deciding that she at least ought to try it out while she had the chance, she carried it down to the driveway and climbed on. It took her a wobbily moment to find the right gear, but an instant later she was speeding down the street.

After the loud grinding of her old bike, the Peugeot was miraculously quiet. As she pedaled effortlessly along it made only a soft, efficient whir. There was a low click as the chain dropped from one gear to the next.

She was tempted to keep it, but as she turned back into the Petersens' driveway, she decided that it would injure her pride to do so. What she wanted was an apology, not a bribe.

"I can't accept it," she said to the young man. "You'll have to take it back."

"I can't do that," the boy said uneasily. "The guy paid cash, so all I can really do is exchange it. If you don't want it, you'll have to speak to your friend."

"But I don't even know who this friend *is,*" she replied, exasperated. "Did he happen to give his name?"

The boy's embarrassment grew visibly more acute. "I'm

sorry, but he didn't. You see, we couldn't take it back; we don't know who to return the money to."

Nicole fumed. It seemed she had been outsmarted. Did the man get his jollies this way, coming from all angles, throwing people into confusion? She was dying to give him a piece of her mind, but as the delivery van backed into the street and drove away, she realized she would probably never have the chance.

She was still seething half an hour later as she sat down at the Petersens' dining room table. Her rent didn't include meals, but Emily was getting into the habit of feeding her as well.

"Oh, pooh. Don't think about it," Emily said when she mentioned the subject. "It's wonderful to have a young face around the house again."

A delicious smell was drifting out from the kitchen, and pangs of hunger slowly supplanted Nicole's annoyance over the bicycle incident. Frank Petersen came in and took his place at the table, his portly figure giving testimony to his wife's culinary skills. Nicole had met him late the night before when he had picked her up at Boston's South Street Station. She had been so exhausted from her day-long train trip however, that she had slept through the hour-long ride to Mannihasset Harbor, but in their short acquaintance she had found him a wholly good-natured individual.

"Hello, Nicky," he began in his pleasant twang. "Now, don't let Emily start force-feeding you, like she does me. She won't be satisfied till everyone in sight is fat as a quahog."

"What nonsense!" Emily exclaimed, sweeping into the room with a steaming tureen. "I never noticed that you needed any persuasion at the dinner table, Frank."

Frank chuckled. "Well, I do think it would be more

than I could bear to see a pretty figure like Nicky's spoiled by your sinful cooking."

Emily passed around large bowls of Portuguese clam stew. The dizzying smell of sausage and fat, tender clams in their garlicy broth of tomatoes and wine, sent her into paroxysms of hunger.

Fifteen minutes later she was pulling the last clam from its shell with her fork and popping it into her mouth with a contented sigh, the events of the day entirely forgotten. Remarkable how a good meal could improve one's disposition!

"Well, what do you think of our poky little town," Frank asked her.

With a twinge of guilt Nicole realized that she hadn't been paying any attention to the conversation. "Oh, I don't think it's poky at all!" she protested. "It's lovely— like something from a coffee-table book. I half think I never want to leave."

"Perhaps you won't," Emily said mysteriously. "There's certainly no lack of excitement, is there?"

Sensing a story coming, Frank raised his eyebrows expectantly. Nicole proceeded to tell him about her encounter with the reckless Mercedes driver and the unexpected delivery of the new bicycle.

"I see you've lost no time in working your charms on our unsuspecting local boys," Frank teased. "Next they'll be bringing you champagne and flowers, diamond rings—"

"N-no, it wasn't like that," Nicole stammered, badly wanting to explain how loathsome her benefactor truly was.

"Now, Frank . . ." his wife warned, seeing her discomfort.

He quickly changed the subject. "Tell me about your job."

Gratefully she launched into an account of her tour of the clubhouse and conversation with Steve Fulton, ending with her apprehensions about James Benton's fearsome reputation.

"Oh, he isn't a bad sort. Demanding, yes . . ." Frank commented.

"You *know* him," Nicole asked, surprised.

"Yes. In fact I work for him. I thought you knew," he said, glancing at his wife. "I'm a designer at Benton Aircraft."

Of course! In a flash Nicole remembered reading the cover article of a recent *Time* magazine about the resurgence of industry in the Northeast. The writer had given high praise to the innovative spirit at Benton Aircraft. Strange that she hadn't made the connection before.

"Ten years ago when old man Benton died and young James took the helm, the company was in a sorry state, I can tell you," Frank was saying. "Military contracts were scarce as hen's teeth as the Vietnam War cooled down, but he refitted the plant for the production of small private jets. I've never seen anyone work so hard in my life—he was everywhere. In two years Benton Aircraft had done a complete turnaround; we've opened up a whole new corporate market. Oh, yes, young James saved this town, all right."

Nicole looked skeptical, somehow unwilling to cast James Benton in the role of hero. "He sounds like a slave driver," she said.

"At times he is," Frank agreed, "and thank goodness. But he knows how to use the carrot as well as the club."

Nicole wasn't reassured, but before she had a chance to question him further, Emily came in with a delicious

44

lemon soufflé. It was the perfect follow-up to the spicy clam stew, and Nicole demolished her portion so quickly that she looked up sheepishly to see if her hosts had noticed her bad manners.

But Frank and Emily were exchanging news.

"He's got me analyzing performance readouts for that darn boat again," Frank was complaining.

"Your boss?" Nicole asked.

"Yes. You've heard of his boat, *Warlord?* Well, lately I've been spending half my time designing new sails for the thing."

In spite of herself Nicole was suddenly interested. Encouraging him, she listened as he explained how *Warlord* had been equipped with a computer. It tabulated data about wind and boat speed, and the readouts were then used to help redesign the sails and plan hull modifications.

"Can you do that kind of thing with your background?" Nicole asked, impressed. "I mean, I wouldn't have thought airplane and boat design were very closely related."

"Close enough," Frank answered. "Sails propel a boat forward in the water in exactly the same way that wings lift an airplane off the ground."

"I'm surprised Benton isn't in the sailing business. Why doesn't he start a boat yard?"

"Not enough money in it, I suppose. His little hobby is horribly expensive and he needs a highly lucrative operation like Benton Aircraft in order to indulge himself the way he does."

Nicole considered this. It certainly was convenient to have a staff of engineers at your disposal for both work and play. Benton had certainly organized his life for maximum efficiency, she thought distastefully. How dull it must be to be a perfectionist!

Later, sitting on the porch in the cool evening breeze, she pondered all that Frank had told her. He obviously put James Benton together in a category with the gods. Steve's portrait had been less complimentary, yet nevertheless it had been unmistakably colored with respect.

Would she be won over by him as well? Probably not. She hated smug success in others. Yet looking at herself objectively, she knew that it was partly her own highly competitive and fiercely independent nature that often made her judge harshly.

Nicole was an only child. Her mother had died when she was very young, leaving her only a few dim memories of a smiling, dark-haired woman gathering her in her arms. Her father had never remarried. He had always provided well for her, but his career in university administration had kept him fully occupied. When he died earlier in the year, she had felt curiously detached, as if he were a stranger.

The most pleasant memories of her childhood were of her annual summer-long visits to a girls camp on the Chesapeake Bay. She had excelled at sailing and spent every available hour out on the water in the camp's tiny dinghies. Once she had even sailed clear across the bay, completely losing sight of the opposite shore. She had been disciplined harshly after that adventure, but at that friendless period in her life the utter solitude of the open water had been her idea of perfect happiness.

Later she had learned to make friends, but even when she was a teen-ager, her aloofness had often been mistaken for snobbery. Her intelligence and competitiveness had scared away most of the boys, which she thought was just as well.

When she reached college, though, her petite good looks had prompted a few of the braver men on campus to ask her out. But none of these relationships had gone beyond the kissing stage. While her friends indulged themselves in the sexual excesses of her generation, Nicole had no trouble holding herself back. No one had been able to touch the iron-bound inner core of passion she kept locked deep within her.

Until now.

The thought slipped into her head quite unexpectedly, but she quickly pushed it out again. She didn't want to think about the warm glow that had spread through her as the dark stranger held her.

Looking up, she noticed that the sun was nearly gone. Long fingers of cloud stretched out from the horizon, tinged with red. They seemed to be stretching toward her, reaching to take her in their fiery, insubstantial grasp.

Now I'm getting morbid, she said laughingly to herself. A deep, luminous blue was settling in above her, and she felt a bone-deep weariness coming over her. Lifting herself from the seductive cushions of her chair, she went indoors.

The next day Nicole had little time for brooding. She spent the better part of the morning in Bensen's Marine, happily lost in the business of choosing paints and supplies. The afternoon found her hunched over a wildly vibrating sanding machine. It was hard, sweaty work, but the day passed quickly. Already three of the dinghies had been stripped and sanded.

The Peugeot brought her speeding back to the Petersens' in time for another dangerously delicious dinner. A long leisurely shower had taken most of the tension out of her aching arms and shoulders, and now she sat in front of her mirror wrapped in a large bath towel, trying to decide how to put her limited collection of makeup to best use.

47

She frowned at her features in the mirror. If only her face weren't so dark and unhappy-looking! Her fashion-conscious college roommate, Andrea, had told her that her puffy, pouting mouth was quite fashionable, and had showed her pictures of several models in *Vogue* to illustrate her point.

When Nicole continued to demur, Andrea had gone to work on her with a formidable array of cosmetics. She had come out looking convincingly like a fashion model herself, but she felt as if her face would crack if she so much as smiled. Andrea encouraged her to experiment with her makeup kit, but Nicole had rarely taken up the offer.

She sighed, running her eyes over her own pitifully small collection. Well, she ought to make an effort, anyway. Play on your natural coloring, Andrea had told her. Nicole looked at her face again, trying to be objective. Her skin glowed with a healthy, early-summer tan. Perhaps it would be best to leave that alone.

Next she considered her dark, smoky eyes. A date had once told her that they made her look sultry, but she had taken this for an insult.

Working quickly, so that she wouldn't have time to reconsider, she applied a charcoal-gray eyeliner, a touch of tan shadow, and a light highlighter. Sitting back to examine the results, she was pleased to find that her eyes seemed twice as large as usual without also looking as if they were encrusted with goo.

Encouraged, she traced her lips with a deep red lipgloss, and pressed her lips together over a tissue, then swept the makeup into a drawer. There. It wasn't much, but it would have to do.

She glanced at the clock on the dresser. Five minutes to eight. Steve would be arriving shortly. Hastily she flung off the towel, stepped into a pair of bikini briefs, and strapped on her thin high-heeled sandals.

Thinking she would need only practical clothes that summer, she had packed only one of her two evening gowns. Now, as she slipped it over her head, she began to regret her choice. It was made of a sheer pale green material that clung to her trim hips and slender legs. The neckline was lower than she would have liked too. Most of her back was exposed and the whole thing was held up by a pair of inadequate-looking spaghetti straps. It was certainly flattering, but she wished she had something more conservative for the occasion.

After carefully brushing her short, shiny hair into place, she sprayed on a hint of perfume, picked up her small satin handbag, and started down the stairs.

Frank, who was leafing through the evening paper, started visibly when he saw her. "Good heavens! What's happened to our sweet, young Nicky!"

"Frank, do stop! Why, you look positively lovely," Emily said from her place on the couch.

Nicole was saved from answering by the sound of the doorbell. If the Petersens were surprised by her appearance, Steve was absolutely shocked. His mouth flapped soundlessly for a moment before he managed to get out a strangled "Wow."

Thoroughly embarrassed and longing for her familiar jeans and T-shirt, Nicole called a quick good-night to the Petersens and started out the door. Recovering himself, Steve ran ahead to hold open the door of his battered station wagon.

Sliding into the driver's seat, he said, "When you're out to make a good impression, you don't kid around, do you?"

Nicole smiled nervously. "What's the matter, sonny? Ain't cha never seen a lady before?" she joked.

"Oh, wait. I almost forgot." After reaching into the backseat, he brought up a florist's box and handed it to her awkwardly. Pulling away a layer of tissue paper, she found a white carnation corsage inside.

"Thank you. How sweet!" Slipping it over her wrist, she leaned over and planted an impulsive kiss on his cheek. Steve turned a noticeable shade of pink, but with the formalities over he seemed to relax. He chatted easily as they drove toward the shore, but it was a one-way conversation.

"Nervous?" he asked.

"Who me?" she returned, trying without success to sound lighthearted.

"Don't worry. You'll knock 'em dead," Steve promised.

If only she could be so certain! The thought of encountering the formidable James Benton had her nearly paralyzed. All too soon they were making their way over the wooden footbridge to the club. The exterior of the building was softly lit, making it seem abnormally large against the deep blue evening sky. A jumble of voices and brassy dance music spilled out into the night. It was an enchanting sight, but Nicole was feeling anything but romantic.

Taking her arm, Steve led her up the steps and inside. The ballroom was jammed. Beautifully turned-out women in long evening gowns and men in expensive-looking tuxedos were clustered together in groups, talking loudly to be heard above the noise of the band. Couples spun and twirled in front of the low stage. Hundreds of brightly colored burgees from yacht clubs around the world hung from the beams in the ceiling.

Enviously Nicole stared at the dozens of stunning gowns. The fashionable shops on Boston's Newbury Street must have been cleaned out that week, she thought. Taking her elbow, Steve led her over to a distinguished-looking silver-haired man standing in the doorway. His face lit up as they approached.

"Steven, my boy! Where did you win this lovely prize?" he said with the trace of an accent.

"Nicky, I'd like you to meet Peter, the club's manager. Peter, this is Nicole Tanner, our sailing instructor for the summer."

"How unfortunate that the summers are so short in this part of the world! I'm delighted to meet you," he said, taking the hand she offered. She was unable to place his accent—was it Italian?—but nevertheless the genuine warmth of his manner immediately put her at ease.

"Thanks," she said, laughing, "but really, you shouldn't be so charming. You'll spoil me rotten!"

"Ah, that would be a pleasure, believe me," Peter countered, formally kissing her hand.

The mischievous gleam in his eye gave him away, however, and Nicole exclaimed, "Now I *know* you're Italian!"

He dropped her hand, looking mortally offended. "*Italian! Dieu,* you wound my pride. If I were Italian, I would already have my hands many places where they should not be! Please, remember that I am a French-Canadian with delicate sensibilities."

"Oops! I'm sorry—" she began.

"Ah, stop! Do not apologize. You will soon get used to my teasing, I promise," he interrupted, smiling.

He spoke with Steve for a few minutes, then turned to her again with a sunny smile. "Come, let me introduce you to some of the members."

Taking her arm, he led her over to a nearby group and began a round of introductions. Soon she was fielding questions right and left from parents of youngsters in the

51

junior sailing program. A tall blond woman who had introduced herself as Patricia Bowman turned to her with a concerned expression.

"Last year the instructor sent the kids out in the middle of a squall. He said it was for the experience, but my twins were terrified. It was all I could do to talk them into taking sailing lessons again this year. You'll be careful about sending them out in bad weather, won't you?"

"It's not something I would do deliberately," Nicole answered diplomatically. "But I do think it's important to know how to handle a boat when heavy weather comes up unexpectedly."

"Yes, that's sensible," Mrs. Bowman said, looking relieved.

They were interrupted by a squat, heavyset man who shouldered his way through the crowd and confronted Nicole. A foul-smelling cigar was clenched in his fist. Was this James Benton at last, she wondered?

"Look, we've got a championship team here and I want you to understand one thing," he said without preamble. "We can't have you wasting your time with namby-pamby beginners when you've got winners to look out for. You follow me?"

"S-sure," Nicole said, taken aback.

"Good! I'll be watching you." With that he wheeled around and strode away.

"Yipe! Who was *that*?" she asked. It could only have been Benton.

Mrs. Bowman grimaced. "That's Sal Wentworth. His son is some sort of hotshot junior sailor. You'll be able to pick him out right away. He's just like his dad."

Nicole shuddered. The evening wore on in a fog of noisy conversation and cigarette smoke. Already tired from a hard day, she felt her energy fading rapidly. Benton had yet to put in an appearance, and the suspense was making her jittery. The two wine spritzers she had gulped down had not helped to settle her nerves.

Muttering an excuse, she detached herself from the group she was in and made her way out to the uncrowded porch. In the clear, outdoor air she immediately felt better. Leaning against the railing, she let the warm breeze wash over her.

It was a beautiful night. Lights twinkled across the harbor, sending lazy streaks across the water. Waves brushed against the rocks below the porch, and in the harbor dozens of yachts bobbed at their moorings. At the end of the breakwater opposite the club, a red beacon stood atop a metal structure blinking on and off at long intervals, marking the entrance to the harbor.

"Daydreaming again, I see," said a familiar voice behind her.

Spinning around, Nicole found herself facing the man who had nearly run her down the day before. What was *he* doing here?

Taken by surprise, she could only stare at him. He was dressed in a crisp, impeccably tailored tuxedo that somehow managed to accentuate his rugged figure. In the soft, shadowy light of the porch his chiseled features were annoyingly handsome.

"I'd have thought you'd learned by now that daydreaming can be dangerous," he teased lightly. "When you're not looking where you're going, you may find yourself in trouble."

"Well, as you can see I'm not going anywhere at the moment," she replied irritably.

"Good," he said. "I've been looking forward to having another chat with you."

She kicked herself mentally for falling into his trap. She

53

had happily accepted the fact that she would never see him again, and his appearance now was both inconvenient and unwelcome. She would have to find a way to end the conversation quickly. "About the bicycle," she began.

"Please, don't mention it," he commanded in his low, masculine voice. "It was no trouble."

Then, before she had a chance to pursue the matter further, his tone became politely inquisitive. "I'm told you're going to tackle the job of turning an unruly mob of kids into crack sailors for us. I'd like to hear about your plans—that is, if you're not yet sick of the subject."

His abrupt change of mood confused her. How was she supposed to tell him off if he made himself agreeable? Now there was no way to get out of the situation without being as rude as he himself had been. Abandoning the sharp remark on the tip of her tongue, she proceeded to describe her ideas for teaching a safe, knowledgeable approach to sailing.

He listened with an intent expression, nodding occasionally. When she had finished, he regarded her thoughtfully for a long moment. Looking up at him, she felt a tingle run down her spine. For the first time since the beginning of the evening, she found herself uncomfortably aware of the expanse of bare skin left exposed by her dress. Damn the man! Why did he have to be so good-looking?

When he finally spoke, his voice was quiet but firm. "You're perfectly right about teaching the theory on shore. There's no sense knowing how if you don't first understand why. But it's also important to be able to react instinctively to, say, a sudden wind shift. That kind of lightning-quick response comes only through repeated practice."

He grew more peremptory as he continued, "The best kind of practice is racing. Lots of it. It's that pressure to succeed, to win, that sharpens the responses and builds an instinctive feel for what to do in any given situation. Constant competition is the best teacher."

Nicole felt her hackles rise. Although she understood his logic, she resented being lectured. "That's a very cynical view," she shot back thoughtlessly.

"Cynical? No, just practical. The rigorous hands-on approach has been used here for a number of years with excellent results, as I'm sure you must know. And that's the way it should remain—"

"Forever more, amen," she put in petulantly. The man really was an impossible bully! What right did he have to criticize her, anyway?

He gave her a look of sharp disapproval but then suddenly changed his tone again. Now he was patiently reasonable, as if he were speaking to a stubborn child. "Look, I just want to make things easier for you. You may think of this as just another summer job, but believe me, you can find yourself under a lot of pressure. And I hate to see a pretty face looking troubled, as I do now."

She quickly forced her features into a neutral expression. Putting a compliment on top of criticism, he had expertly cut off the retort she was about to make.

"Actually the summer can be quite pleasant here if you choose to enjoy it," he continued. "Have you seen the view from the balcony? No? May I show you?"

Without giving her time to object, he took her arm and began leading her toward the stairs at the end of the porch. Surprisingly she found that she didn't mind. After an exhausting evening of questions and scrutiny it was pleasant to be treated with consideration . . . even if it was only temporary, she thought wryly.

When they reached the balcony, they found it deserted. He led her to a railing overlooking the ocean. The faraway noise of the ballroom mingled enchantingly with the sound of waves washing against the shore. The three-quarter moon had just risen to throw a pale silvery light over the scene.

They stood in silence for a moment, breathing in the clean sea air. Nicole found herself unexpectedly relaxed. Perhaps it was the wine . . . or was she simply tired from her long day? It certainly couldn't have had anything to do with Mr. Mercedes. . . .

Suddenly she realized that she didn't know his name. She turned to him, but the question caught in her throat. Leaning on one elbow, he had been studying her with unashamed interest.

From the sparkle in his eye she was certain that he was enjoying her discomfort, but he spoke with disarming kindness. "Pardon me for being so didactic a moment ago. That was rather thoughtless of me. No doubt you're a bit nervous being thrust into these new surroundings."

"A bit," she admitted, dropping her eyes.

"I wouldn't worry. You may lack a certain degree of . . . experience, but I'm sure you're quite capable."

Before she was able to decide whether this was another of his veiled insults, he stepped close to her and slowly raised her chin with his fingertips. As she looked into his bottomless, dark eyes, alarm bells began going off in her head.

She sensed what he was about to do, but the strength had mysteriously drained out of her limbs. Caught in a confusing whirl of panic and desire, she stood frozen as he bent his head toward her.

His kiss was soft at first, a gentle questioning. Then, as his hands came to rest lightly on her shoulders, his lips grew more insistent. She felt herself responding hesitantly.

It was her undoing. Recognizing his advantage, he

pulled her close to him as his mouth came crushing down on hers with fearsome deliberation. Nicole felt her already weakened impulse to resist go spinning away in the vortex of this sensual assault. Helpless against the strength of her own desires, she pressed her body against his, quivering with fear and discovery.

Expertly his arms locked around her, trapping her. His restless mouth explored hers for an eternity, forcing her lips apart. She was dizzy with the feeling of his moist lips moving across hers, his intoxicating masculine scent, the material of his suit pressing against her bare skin.

But then came a shrill warning from some deep reserve of self-preservation. Suddenly, with every ounce of will-power she could summon, she brought her hands up and pushed against him.

Abruptly he released her. As she stumbled back, gasping for breath, she saw a string of reactions flick across his face. What finally settled there was a light, ironic smile. Casually he slipped his hands in his trouser pockets.

As if nothing at all had happened, he said easily, "Yes, a bit inexperienced, but quite capable just the same."

A furious cry of humiliation jumped from her throat. What absolute, burning gall! He had laid a vicious trap for her, and she had let him lead her straight into it. How could she have been so stupid?

Flushing deeply, she managed to say, "Yes, I'm capable of knowing an insult when I hear one, anyway."

With that she wheeled around deliberately and marched down the stairs. Bursting with rage and self-reproach, she hurried into the safety of the crowded ballroom. With relief she saw that the music had stopped and all attention was focused on the stage, where Peter was speaking into a microphone.

Quietly she slipped to the back of the room, hoping her

cheeks didn't look as hot as they felt. After a minute she had composed herself enough to listen to what was happening.

Peter was announcing details of the summer's social calendar, his accent more pronounced as it came through the speakers. ". . . and of course the dinning room will be open every evening from six o'clock until the hour of midnight. Though you won't find *me* there at that hour, as it is long past my bedtime."

A wave of polite laughter came from the crowd. As it fell off, Peter looked anxiously around the room, saying, "And now I'm afraid I can no longer delay the introduction of our . . . ah, *elusive* commodore, Mr. James Benton. James, I hope you are there!"

There was a burst of clapping. Suddenly alert, Nicole stood on tiptoe, stretching to see above the tall heads in front of her. At last the mysterious Benton was going to show himself. She wanted a good look at her new boss.

An athletic figure detached itself from the crowd and hopped neatly onto the stage.

For a moment she couldn't believe her eyes. But then the reality of what she was seeing hit her like a physical blow. Adjusting the microphone stand to accommodate his height was the man who had been kissing her wildly just a few minutes before!

There was no hint in the cool, collected figure on stage of the scene that had just ended on the balcony. He began speaking in the authoritative voice she knew so well. "Good evening, and welcome once again to another fun-filled summer at Camp Watch Point."

The crowd laughed, but Nicole smoldered, unhearing. A vocabulary of invective that she didn't knew she possessed came to her as she silently cataloged his offensiveness. God, how she hated him! How could these people listen so attentively to him . . . ?

With a start she realized that he was introducing the staff. ". . . glad to have Mr. Steve Fulton acting as dockmaster once again," he said.

The enthusiastic applause that followed this testified to Steve's popularity with the membership. When it died down, Benton spoke again, though his voice was now noticeably cool.

"Lastly, our sailing instructor for the season. I'm afraid the fellow that we hired originally had to abandon us at the last moment. In my absence the Junior Sailing Committee has broken with tradition and hired Miss Nicole Tanner, and with her I'm sure we'll make do."

There was hesitant applause, but Nicole shrank back. More than anything she wanted to crawl under a table of hors d'oeuvres and disappear. Her cheeks flamed more hotly than before. Were there no lengths to which he wouldn't go to insult her? His introduction had been distinctly patronizing.

Mercifully the official ceremonies were soon over. Smoldering with anger, Nicole searched the room for Steve. The sooner they got out of there, the better, she thought.

She found him talking with Peter. As she approached Steve said tactlessly, "That wasn't exactly a sparkling introduction, was it?"

"Would you mind taking me home now?" she asked. If only she could rewind time and erase this whole evening!

"Don't run away yet" came James's commanding voice from behind her.

She turned to confront him with sparks in her eyes. "Was there something more you wanted to discuss?"

"Oh, I see you two have met already," Peter exclaimed,

clearly disappointed that he had not been the one to make the introduction.

"Oh, yes. We've grown . . . close in a very short space of time," James said smoothly. Turning back to Nicole, he said, "In fact there was one more item of business I wanted to discuss before we were, ah, interrupted. Since we won't have time to cover all the details this evening, I'd like you to type out an outline of your proposed program and bring it to me at my office. Shall we say the day after tomorrow at eleven o'clock? Steve can tell you where it is."

His imperious tone made her blood boil. Not trusting herself to speak, she looked toward Steve, who nodded his head in compliance.

Fortunately they were interrupted at that moment by the approach of an unmistakably feminine figure. Although Nicole judged the woman to be about her own age, she looked much older. She had a mass of silver-blond hair and wore a good deal of expertly applied makeup. Her provocative body was displayed in a dress revealing enough for the cover of *Cosmopolitan*.

Without apology she wrapped herself around James's arm and whined, "Jimmy, it was perfectly rude of you to leave me with that boring dry-cleaning person. You are very bad!"

Without waiting for an answer, she looked around at the others as if noticing them for the first time. "Now I suppose you are going to refuse to introduce me to these people," she complained.

Coolly James said, "I believe you've already met Peter and Steve. This is Nicole Tanner. Nicole, Sheilah Pritchard."

"How do you do," Nicole said. Sheilah ignored her. With a toss of her head she flipped back her abundant hair over her shoulder and looked up at James with babylike eyes. "Why don't you come dance with me?"

Looking discouraging, James was about to reply when Nicole seized her chance. "Please, don't let me take up any more of your time. I was just going in any case. Good night."

With that she grabbed Steve's arm and pulled him toward the door, saying a rapid good-bye to the amused-looking Peter.

It wasn't until she was safely home at the Petersens', vigorously scrubbing the makeup from her face, that she remembered that she had been commanded to appear in Benton's office in two days.

Damn! She would have preferred never to see him again in her life, though she knew this was not possible. He had certainly gone out of his way to make a fool of her, and she would have told him off on the spot if she hadn't needed this job so desperately.

Conflicting thoughts and images swirled around in her tired brain, but one fact stood out clearly: Steve had said she would have a head-on collision with Benton and he had been right—in more ways than one!

CHAPTER 3

Thanks to Steve's directions it took Nicole only twenty minutes to make her way out to an industrial park outside of town on the appointed morning. Except for the tidy factory buildings isolated in their landscaped grounds, this area of the countryside was undeveloped. Birds chattered noisily, and the air was fresh with the clean smell of dry grass.

Although the Peugeot carried her along effortlessly, she still felt uncomfortably hot. She had worn a light pin-striped cotton shirtdress and her everyday sandals in the hope of keeping cool, but the midmorning sun burned through the thin material on her back.

The blinking yellow traffic lights at the entrance to each factory seemed to be cautioning her, warning her away from the coming meeting with James. Wishing it were over already, she peered ahead. Heat shimmered off the black surface of the road, but Benton Aircraft was not yet in sight.

Then, from somewhere off to her right, came a low,

ominous roar. It rapidly grew to a deafening pitch, until a small jet burst above a clump of trees, screaming overhead not a hundred feet off the ground.

Nicole ducked involuntarily. The noise died away quickly, leaving her feeling a bit foolish and even more jittery than she had already.

As she rounded a bend an airfield came into view, enclosed behind a chain-link fence that seemed to stretch down the road forever. Off in the distance she could see an imposing cluster of buildings, topped by a low control tower and a spinning radar dish. A sign with shiny steel letters announced, Benton Aircraft Corporation.

At last she reached the entrance gate, where a young uniformed guard was seated on a stool reading a paperback. She asked for the executive offices, and he pointed her toward a nearby building, adding, "We could use some more like you around here. I hope you get the job!"

Yeah, me too, she thought to herself unhappily as she wheeled the bike across the parking lot. The sight of the killer Mercedes, no worse for wear, parked in a reserved space close to the doors, only increased her dread of the coming interview.

Without giving herself time for further reflection, she locked the bike, pulled her lesson outline from the snaprack over the back wheel, and marched quickly through the dark glass doors. Inside, the reception area was sparsely furnished with oddly shaped ultramodern furniture units and exotic plants.

"Just have a seat over there, dear, and try to relax," said the woman behind the reception desk when she explained her errand. The woman pushed three numbers on her telephone console.

Nicole perched on what she supposed was a chair and tried to compose herself. She certainly didn't want to let

James know that he had pushed her off balance by forcing her to come to these unfamiliar surroundings.

The receptionist put down her receiver and said, "Someone will be with you in just a minute."

That's okay, make it an hour, she said silently, glancing toward a door marked AUTHORIZED PERSONNEL ONLY. Nervously she wondered what new tactics he would try on her today. Would he be cordial, letting the cowed, obsequious manner of his employees be an example for her? No, that would be too subtle. Blunt threats were more his style.

Before she could go any further with this line of thought, the inner door opened and out stepped Frank Petersen, a plastic identification card clipped to his shirt pocket.

"Hello there, Nicky!" he called as she jumped up with a smile of pleasure. "Guess what? Young James is going to be tied up in a meeting for a bit, so mercifully he unchained me from my desk and ordered me to show you around. What luck!"

Nicole gave him a peck on the cheek and said, "Ah! Rescued just in the nick of time!"

Leading her back out the front door, Frank asked, "Have you ever seen heavy assembly work before?" When she shook her head, he joked, "Well, then, I'll do my best to keep you totally bewildered."

Nicole laughed again. For the next hour he led her through a maze of interconnected work areas. Some, like the electronics assembly area, were quiet and subdued. Others were unbelievably noisy, like the main shop floor, where half-finished jet bodies stood in rows like streamlined dinosaur skeletons. Rowdy workers whistled and banged their toolboxes when they saw her.

Frank turned to her, his eyes bright with amusement.

"If we have a drop in the day's production rate, we'll know who to blame," he said.

She felt awkward and conspicuous wearing a dress in the midst of so many comfortable-looking overalls. But she gamely followed Frank, listening as he explained how models were tested in the wind tunnel. The jet she had seen earlier was coming in from its test flight, and they followed its progress on the confusing array of scopes and screens in the control tower.

The entire plant was immaculate and well-organized, painted in bright, invigorating colors. In each department Nicole noticed that management offices weren't segregated from the rest of the work area. More often than not they were anonymous cubicles.

When she asked Frank about this, he said, "That's because we believe management should be intimately involved with day-to-day operations."

She didn't need to ask from whom *that* idea had come. "Intimately involved": that probably meant bullying and browbeating the workers. She kept this thought to herself, however.

All too soon he was leading her through the quiet halls of the administration wing with their distinctive smell of stationery and stale coffee. A few twists and turns brought them to an open doorway labeled simply JAMES E. BENTON. Thanking him, Nicole watched Frank disappear back down the hall like the last lifeboat from a sinking ship.

Then, taking a deep breath, she turned and walked through the door.

She was immediately arrested dead in her tracks by a pair of flashing icy blue eyes aimed at her from behind a secretary's desk. A silver-colored nameplate identified their owner as Ms. Jackie Faulkner.

Taken aback by Ms. Faulkner's hard, disapproving stare, Nicole searched for something to say. The woman's expression seemed to suggest that the best course of action would be to turn around and go back the way she had come.

Finally, though, she summoned her courage and said as coolly as she could manage, "I have an appointment with Mr. Benton."

"Name?" Ms. Faulkner asked matter-of-factly.

"Nicole Tanner."

"Just a moment." She consulted a book on her desk.

Nervously Nicole shifted her weight from one foot to the other and looked around the room. It was furnished less aggressively than the reception area. A comfortable-looking sofa stood against one wall and opposite it was a floor-to-ceiling window overlooking the airfield and the woods beyond. A few modest photographs of small jets hung on the walls—hardly the shrine to James Benton's achievements she had been expecting.

Ms. Faulkner was taking a long time with her appointment calendar. Just as Nicole began to imagine that her feet were sending down roots into the beige carpet, the secretary looked up and resumed her critical appraisal once again.

"Please have a seat," she commanded. "We'll fit you in when we can."

Gratefully Nicole sank down on the sofa and mentally began to review the outline she had prepared. After a few minutes she felt her courage returning. The outline was logical, complete, and well-organized. Surely he couldn't require any more than that.

She shifted her legs and looked around the room again. Behind her desk Ms. Faulkner was absorbed in her typing. Her fingers flew over the keys with impressive speed.

Nicole glanced at her watch. She had been waiting for fifteen minutes, and there was still no indication of when James would see her.

She looked around for some distraction. No magazines were provided, so instead she studied Ms. Faulkner. From the woman's profile she could see that she had the gaunt good looks her high-fashion outfit demanded. Shining brown hair tumbled to her shoulders in a mass of loose curls. She had to have spent an hour on her makeup alone.

Nicole experienced a pang of inadequacy. She had never bothered to devote so much time to her looks, and although her figure was satisfyingly trim, she felt plain and girlish by comparison. At least she could match the woman's healthy tan.

Idly she wondered if Jackie Faulkner was another of his willing conquests. Probably, she thought, as she quickly suppressed a twinge of jealousy.

James Benton was clearly not her type, she told herself. A voice in the back of her head insisted that she didn't know what her type was, but she conveniently ignored it.

She glanced at her watch again. Forty minutes had gone by. What was holding him up, anyway?

Reluctantly Nicole stood up and walked over to the secretary's desk. "Excuse me," she inquired. "Do you know when Mr. Benton will be able to see me?"

Jackie Faulkner looked up at her, her eyes flashing. "No, I do not! We have a number of *important* matters to see to this morning and we'll get to you when we can. Now, please remain seated," she said sharply.

Stinging from this needless rebuff, Nicole marched back to the sofa and threw herself down, fuming silently. How entirely rude! If she were a man, she was sure she wouldn't have been kept waiting for more than a minute or two. If he was trying to put her in her place, then his plan was backfiring badly.

To make matters worse, her stomach was beginning to growl. It was lunchtime, and hunger contributed to her growing fury.

Studying her short nails, she tried to remain calm. Outside, a jet flashed past the window, roaring down the runway for takeoff. She looked toward Ms. Faulker menacingly, but she was at her typewriter again, her blood-red nails jabbing the keys furiously.

When an hour and twenty minutes had elapsed, Nicole felt ready to explode. She was certain that Benton had forgotten her altogether and she was steeling herself for another confrontation with Ms. Faulkner when the secretary abruptly snapped off her typewriter, took her matching jacket from the back of her chair, and walked out of the office without a word.

Nicole was incredulous. This was too much! She had just decided to write an angry note and leave when the door to the inner office opened and James Benton stepped out.

"Jackie . . ." he began. Seeing that his sentry was gone, he turned to go back to his office. Only then did he spot Nicole.

"Oh, you're here," he said nonchalantly. "Why don't you come in?"

Slowly she rose from the sofa and followed him into his office, wondering whether she should express her annoyance. The best thing would be to say nothing, she decided. Letting him know that the long wait had had the desired effect would only earn her further scorn.

She looked around his uncluttered office, trying to see what had kept him busy for nearly an hour and a half. The

68

top of his vast desk was clean except for a telephone. Near it stood a chalkboard with an unidentifiable shape drawn on it, surrounded by mathematical equations that meant nothing to her.

He motioned her into a chair and circled around his desk, moving with a distracting animal grace. He was wearing navy slacks and a fitted shirt that stretched across the muscles of his chest. His silk tie was pulled down, and a few dark chest hairs curled up where his collar was unbuttoned.

Sinking into his chair, he fixed his eyes on her and said unexpectedly, "My, you're a refreshing sight. You make me think of all the places I'd rather be right now."

Confused by this compliment, Nicole did not reply, but only stared at him. She felt anything but refreshing.

He regarded her with a puzzled expression for a moment, then said in a businesslike tone, "Have you done your homework? Good, let me see it."

She handed it to him across his desk and retreated quickly back to her chair. Somehow she was glad to have the barrier of his desk between them.

As he shuffled through her outline she furtively studied his face. Its solid, angular features could have been hewed from the ancient granite of the New England coast, and yet there were contradictory qualities to it. Its ruggedness was balanced by intelligence, and something there suggested tenderness or compassion, as if the sculptor had only blocked out the main dimensions, leaving it rough and unfinished.

Suddenly James looked up, catching her staring at him. He seemed to take no notice, though.

"This seems fairly complete," he said. "I expect you've taken into account our brief discussion the other night?"

"Of course." As if she had any choice in the matter!

"Then I don't imagine I'll find too much to quarrel with here. We'll discuss it at greater length when I've had a chance to go through it carefully. Thank you."

"Couldn't we go through it now?" she asked, startled. She hadn't waited an hour and a half for a thirty-second interview!

"No, I'm afraid we can't, as it is now rather late. I have a lunch conference coming up shortly. I'll show you out," he offered, rising.

"No! I can find my own way out," she blurted. Suddenly the room seemed suffocating. She rose from her seat and strode out without a backward glance. Furious, she marched down the hall, preoccupied with her hostile thoughts.

How utterly loathsome he was. And what a talent for ingenuous insults! One would have thought that it was her fault that time had run short.

It was a full fifteen minutes before she managed to find her way out to the parking lot. More angry than ever, she went speeding across the parking lot and out the gate, leaving the openmouthed guard staring after her.

Several hours later Nicole had changed into her work clothes—an old pair of jeans and a paint-spattered T-shirt —but her anger had not diminished. She shoved the electric sander across an upside-down dinghy hull with a vengeance, pretending it was James Benton.

Paint dust flew into the air, blanketing the immediate vicinity with a fine white film. Seeing Steve approach, she switched off the sander and raised her safety goggles. The clean ring of skin around her eyes contrasted oddly with the rest of her face.

"You look like a raccoon!" Steve laughed.

"Oh, yeah? *You* look like you're underworked. How about giving me a hand?" she retorted.

"I suppose I could do that. How'd it go with Benton?"

Delighted that he had asked, Nicole related the story of her minimeeting with the great demigod, punctuating her speech with angry gestures.

Steve was unimpressed. "Typical," he snorted. "Where's that other sander?"

The work went quickly with Steve helping, and by late afternoon they had finished the last of the sanding. After helping her rig two dinghies whose paint had survived the winter without blistering, Steve returned to his own chores.

Standing on the gas dock, Nicole examined the two finished dinghies as they bobbed in the water. Noticing their loose shrouds, she pressed her lips thoughtfully. She took a large screwdriver to use as a lever and stepped into the nearest boat and began methodically tightening its turnbuckles.

Absorbed in this task, she didn't hear the approaching footsteps. Suddenly she was startled by a cough behind her. She spun around and the screwdriver fell from her hand, clattering to the floor of the dinghy.

Looming above her with his arms folded was James.

"Do try to keep a grip on your tools," he said sarcastically. "They're no use when dropped overboard—not to mention the replacement cost."

"What do you expect when you come sneaking up on people like that?" she shot back. It was trouble enough keeping a grip on her temper!

"Ah, but you should always be on the lookout for your opponents," he said lightly. "That is, if that is how you wish to regard me."

She was uncertain how to reply. Did she really want an

adversary relationship with him? Oddly her pent up anger seemed to be fading.

Since she had last seen him, he had changed into a pair of khaki pants and a white cotton sport shirt that contrasted handsomely with his tanned skin. She felt grubby by comparison and hastily raised an arm to wipe away the perspiration from her forehead.

"Did you want to discuss the outline?" she asked, avoiding his last remark.

"Yes, if you'll climb out of there."

Dusting off her jeans, she stood and hopped up to the gunwale of the dinghy. As her foot stretched for the dock, however, the boat moved backward underneath her. Leaping awkwardly, she stumbled onto the dock.

Instantly James reached out, catching her. Then, with astonishing ease, he lifted her to her feet. For a thrilling instant they were only inches apart. Her heart hammered in her chest and she caught the faint smell of his spicy after-shave.

Panicking, she stepped backward and nearly fell off the dock. His strong hands steadied her, though, and he broke into a broad grin.

"Whoa there! I'm beginning to think you're accident prone."

"I'm not!" she declared, breaking away from him. "At least not always," she added. She could hardly tell him that it was his distracting presence that turned her into a fumbling boob.

"So you wanted to go over the program," she said to cover her embarrassment.

"Yes." He crossed his arms. "I've read it over carefully. It's logically thought out and well presented, but it's too limited. You've allocated too much time for shore classes and not enough for practice races. You must realize that once they've grasped the basic maneuvers, the kids will automatically improve as they go along."

"Okay, I'll buy that," she said grudgingly. "What else?"

"With the advanced classes you haven't paid enough attention to strategy and tactics," he continued in the same severe tone. "You've completely forgotten things like downwind tacking and mark-rounding drills. The program will have to be expanded."

He went on to review her outline from memory, lesson by lesson, pausing often to comment critically. Nicole clenched her teeth, somehow unwilling to admit that his remarks were all justified. At last she could stand his authoritarian manner no longer.

"What would you know about it?" she exploded. Suddenly the full fury of the past few days came rushing back to her. She pounced on his criticism of a session of tacking drills. "When was the last time you had to handle the sheets during a tack, anyway? Because you have a dozen people to do it for you, you don't think it's important."

His darkening expression should have warned her to stop, but she went on with heedless sarcasm. "You think money will solve all your problems for you. Not going fast enough? Buy new sails! Get a computer to figure out the answers for you! But for heaven's sake don't dirty your hands with the simple things that really matter."

All at once she realized what she was doing. Her rage vanished like smoke in a strong breeze. Here she was arguing with her employer her first week on the job! Flying off the handle was the last thing likely to impress a cool-headed operator like James.

Forcing herself to look at him, she saw that the damage was already done. He was studying her with cool malice.

"Actually I can see your point," he said unexpectedly. "You have every right to question my authority in this

73

area, having no evidence of my competence." His tone was reasonable, but there was a malicious gleam in his eye.

He went on, "What I'd suggest, then, is that you give me a chance to prove myself. A short race would do the trick. Conveniently we have two equally matched dinghies at hand, so if you'll pull out two sets of sails, I'll go find Steve and have him run the starting sequence for us."

Fear gripped her heart. He was challenging her to a race! No, it wasn't a challenge. It was a command. And because of her ill-considered outburst she didn't dare refuse. Backing out would only double the damage.

Moving like an automaton, she fetched mainsails, jibs, and spinnakers from their storage room, stopping to wash the dust from her face and arms. *You've done it now!* she thought ruefully as she dried herself off. How could she hope to beat him? Race him or not, she was a loser either way.

Back at the dock Steve had appeared. He gave her a questioning look, but there was no opportunity to explain to him.

"Wh-what's the course going to be?" she asked, not quite able to keep the tremor from her voice.

"The starting line will be between the flagpole and the end of the breakwater," James said. "Steve will sound an airhorn for a six-minute starting sequence. We'll go upwind to the Ely Island bell buoy, reach to the Pond Point nun, then run back downwind to the starting line. The marks are all within sight of each other. That's fair, don't you agree?"

"Fine," she said, regaining a little confidence. The course was a short one. James Benton might be a world-class champion, but she was a crack sailor herself and she stood a good chance of keeping up with him over a short distance.

When they were both rigged and ready, Steve cast them off and they tacked around the clubhouse toward the starting line. With the wind in her hair and the tiller in her hand, Nicole felt a rush of exhilaration. Expertly she checked the trim of the sails, hauling in on the sheets to bring herself on the wind.

The afternoon breeze was stiff and the little dinghy healed over, sending her scrambling to the windward gunwale to balance it. As they approached the starting line they heard the blast of an airhorn.

Nicole set her watch. Six minutes to go.

She had sailed in many one-on-one match races before and knew exactly what to do. But so did James, and in a minute they were warily circling around each other, each looking for an advantage.

Luck favored her, and with only fifteen seconds left before the start, she seized her chance. Executing a sharp tack, she went speeding toward the line and hit it just as Steve's horn sounded.

She glanced back. James was right behind her, his bow overlapping her stern by a foot or two.

She had him! An electric thrill raced through her. Sailing in her slip stream, he could only fall back. The sails hid him from view, but she could well imagine the look of black concentration on his face. Now she'd show him!

Sure enough, she was soon several boat-lengths ahead. James executed a lightning-quick tack, trying to break away from her. But Nicole was watching him with hawk eyes and tacked to cover his move immediately.

The first leg of the race, zigzagging into the wind, was the most crucial, she knew. The lead established here would only be exaggerated during the rest of the race. If only she could stay in front until the first mark, she was sure to beat him.

Cleverly James led her into a tacking duel, rapidly changing direction back and forth in an attempt to shake her off.

Just as quickly Nicole countered his every move. This was what she liked best in the world: the rippling of her shirt against her skin, the smell of varnish and salt air, the thunderous snapping of the Dacron sails as she crossed the wind—all these things fired her will. Matching wits on the chessboard of the sea made her come alive.

James was also a master player, however, and her triumph was short-lived. An opportune wind shift separated them, and a hundred yards from the bell buoy he crossed in front of her on the opposite tack.

Nicole cursed her luck. All she could do was to stay on her course and hope that the wind would shift back and carry her around the mark ahead of him.

As they approached the bobbing red bell buoy from opposite directions, it looked close. But James went around first, with Nicole not ten seconds behind him.

Furiously she let out her sails, trimming them for the reach to the next mark. As the clanging of the bell buoy faded behind them, she felt her spirits sag. It would be almost impossible to pass him now that they were sailing in a straight line, but if she could get close enough, she just might be able to force him to let her go around the next mark inside of him.

The Pond Point nun buoy was a tiny red speck off in the distance and she headed straight for it. Anxiously she trimmed the sails again and shifted her weight forward, trying everything she could think of to gain speed.

James was sailing a course closer to shore, below the direct line to the mark. After a few minutes she noticed that he was pulling farther ahead. How could that be? Their boats were evenly matched, equipped identically.

Then came a moment of horrible realization. Of course, the tide! He was sailing in the weaker current near shore. She couldn't possibly have known about this aberration in local conditions, and now it was too late to change her course.

As they approached the nun buoy she scrambled around the boat, preparing to raise the spinnaker for the downwind run to the finish line. If only she could get close enough to him on the next leg, she might be able to block his wind with her sails.

With a sinking heart she watched him go around the mark fifty yards ahead of her. An instant later she saw his spinnaker being pulled up out of its bag on the foredeck. The large red, white, and blue sail ballooned out in front of the boat, and he went surging ahead.

Come on! Come on! she silently urged her boat, as if willpower could propel it along faster. Slowly she drew toward the mark. When she reached it, she flipped the boat around it and rushed forward, yanking on the spinnaker halyard to raise the sail into the air.

When it had gone up as far as it could, she looked up in dismay. The colorful red and yellow sail was flapping madly, tangled in a useless hourglass shape.

Damn! She hadn't repacked the spinnaker before leaving the dock. But neither had James. Was it possible that he had done this while concentrating on the race at the same time?

She untangled the mess as quickly as she could, but by the time she had the sail flying right, James was more than halfway to the finish line. She would never catch him now!

She cursed her bad luck, then cursed herself. It was as if James had cast a spell on her, causing her always to do the wrong thing. How could she let herself fall into yet another of his traps?

He had known he would win. Her anger flared, but knowing he had acted deliberately did nothing to diminish her humiliation.

By the time she was halfway to the finish line, James's dinghy had already crossed and disappeared around the distant clubhouse. Damn the man!

CHAPTER 4

When she finally rounded the clubhouse and drifted up to the gas dock, her sails luffing, she was relieved to find that James was nowhere in sight. His dinghy was tied up, its sails neatly folded into their blue nylon bags. As she was securing her own boat to the dock, Steve emerged from his office, holding a white envelope.

Seeing her bleak look, he said, "Don't worry, he's gone."

"Oh, Steve. I feel like such a jerk," she moaned, sinking down on the dock.

Steve sat down beside her. "Cheer up. You were hustled by a pro. I'm only surprised you agreed to race him at all."

"I was asking for it," she said, cupping her chin in her hand. She went on to explain her outburst and how James had adroitly backed her into a situation from which she could not have extricated herself.

"Was he very mad when he came in?" she asked when she had finished.

"No. As a matter of fact he seemed rather pleased. Very unusual for him."

Of course he would look pleased. Everyone liked to win. Especially when it required little effort.

"He did ask me to give you this, though." Steve handed her an envelope.

Her walking papers, probably, she thought miserably. With shaking hands she tore it open and unfolded the single sheet of paper inside. It was a note written in a bold, masculine hand.

It read: *Remember, in every race there is only one winner.*

As she sat at dinner with the Petersens that night, Nicole pondered the meaning of his words. In one way it was simply a restatement of his cynical philosophy. Yet in another it was an entirely personal message . . . but what, precisely?

Somehow that possibility seemed worse than the first, and she quickly forced it out of her mind. No, they were destined to clash. He expected meek obedience, but she was too independent for that. Even when he was right, she chafed as he delivered his commands.

"You're awfully quiet tonight, Nicky." Frank's voice broke into her thoughts. "And you've hardly touched your dinner. Are you not feeling well?"

It was true. Emily had prepared a delicious lasagna, but she had only picked at it.

"I'm fine. Just a little preoccupied," she explained. "If you don't mind, I think I'll skip dessert."

As the Petersens watched with concern, she rose from the table and went dragging out of the room. Upstairs she flopped down on her bed, closed her eyes, and tried to force her mind into neutral territory.

Try as she might, she could not erase the memory of her

humiliation that afternoon. Her face flushed as she remembered her hopelessly tangled spinnaker. She might as well have raised a banner proclaiming, "I am incompetent!" If James wanted to replace her, she had handed him the perfect excuse.

The specter of unemployment loomed over her. What would she do if she was fired? Now that her father was gone, she had no home. She could look for temporary work in New York, but how would she get there in the first place? Her improvident father had left her nothing, and she had used the last of her meager savings to get to Mannihasset Harbor.

She was still agonizing a few minutes later when she heard Emily calling her.

Wearily she pushed herself off the bed and went downstairs. When she reached the living room, she stopped dead, staring in disbelief.

Settled comfortably in one of the easy chairs was James. He was dressed as she had seen him that afternoon, and his thick dark hair was still attractively tousled from the wind. He was chatting with Frank but stopped to study her.

Before either of them could speak, Frank scolded her. "Nicky, here I was imagining it was Emily's cooking that had you in a state. You didn't tell me our mutual employer would be stopping by."

"But I didn't—"

"We're going to deal with some unfinished business on a sight-seeing drive," James cut in hastily. Turning to her again he said, "You'd better bring a sweater along. It may get chilly later."

It's freezing cold right now, she thought unhappily. She hesitated for a moment, but the look he gave her clearly indicated that he would tolerate no objections. She went

81

hurrying back to her room, telling herself that she was playing along only to avoid making a scene in front of the Petersens.

She changed into a clean blouse and knotted a loose-knit sweater around her neck. Pausing at her mirror, she carefully brushed her hair. She was considering applying lipgloss when she brought herself up short. There was no reason to care how she looked for him.

She replaced her brush and went back downstairs. James was waiting for her in the hall.

"Let's go," he ordered.

As they wound their way toward the shore she desperately tried to gather her wits. She would have to attempt to salvage her job, she knew, but she was determined to do it without groveling.

It was hard to think rationally, though, when James was sitting only a foot or two away. She tried to focus her attention on the scenery, but in the enclosed quiet of his car she was uncomfortably aware of every tiny sound: the crunching of the upholstery as he shifted his weight, the ominous ticking of the dashboard clock.

They drove along the shore for several miles, when at last James brought the car to a halt near a deserted beach. The sun had just gone down and the sky was a deep, iridescent blue.

Shutting off the engine, he turned to her. "As I was saying earlier, I think you'll need to have an extra session on starting tactics. Most junior sailors don't really understand the techniques, so our team will have an appreciable advantage if . . ."

Nicole shook her head to be sure she was hearing correctly. He had resumed their conversation at the point where she had made her ill-considered outburst, as if their match race had not taken place.

82

So he wasn't going to fire her after all! Oddly this somehow failed to relieve her apprehensions.

"Do you follow me?" he was asking.

"I—I . . . no, that is—" she stumbled.

"Am I going too fast for you?" he asked without sarcasm.

"No . . . I mean, yes. I'm sorry, it's just that this wasn't what I was expecting."

He raised an eyebrow. "It would be amusing for me to speculate about what you *were* expecting, but perhaps you'd better tell me straight out."

"The fact is, I thought you were going to fire me," she answered honestly.

"But why would I do that?" The surprise in his voice was genuine. "Wait, let me guess. Did you think that because I beat you in a scratch race—in dinghies you had never sailed before, in waters with which you were totally unfamiliar—that I would judge you incompetent?"

"Yes, I—"

"You thought I would settle for nothing less than perfection."

"Yes." When it was put that way, her fears did seem unreasonable. There had really been no reason for her to expect the worst from him. What a child he must think her!

"I see my reputation precedes me once again," he said. "Listen, Nicole, it was highly unlikely that you would have beaten me today."

"Ah, you tricked me deliberately!"

"Yes," he admitted, "though I think you'll agree that you were asking for a takedown. Still, my motives weren't entirely malicious, you know. I was curious to find out what kind of sailor you are."

"And . . . ?"

83

"Begging for compliments now, eh? Well, I will tell you I got a shock. I owe you congratulations: you gave me a real run for my money on that upwind leg."

This was completely unexpected. Disarmed, she could find nothing to say.

"Do I surprise you?" he asked. "Well, don't get too sure of yourself. You'll find me hard to outwit on the water. After all, I've had a good deal more experience than you."

Experience. She remembered with alarm what had happened the last time *that* subject had come up.

Hastily she said, "I thought you would be prejudiced against me. You didn't have an opportunity to interview me, after all."

"I'll confess I was a bit annoyed with the committee for hiring you without waiting to consult me, even though they had little choice. However, once I saw your résumé, I was fairly certain they had made a sound choice. And I see I was right."

Nicole was thrown into confusion. She had suffered terrible humiliation at his hands twice that day, yet now he was treating her with perfect civility. The change that had come over him seemed absolute.

"Let's get some fresh air," he suggested, and for the next hour they strolled down the beach, discussing plans for her classes. When she tentatively put forward some suggestions of her own, he gave them careful consideration. Those with which he disagreed he rejected with faultless diplomacy.

The moon rose higher in the sky and eventually the subject exhausted itself. Their conversation became more general. James was an attentive listener, and his own remarks showed him to be profoundly thoughtful—not at all the bossy, insensitive type she had supposed him.

"That's why I'm bothering to spend time improving this

program with you," he was saying as they wandered back the way they had come. "I believe that when we undertake the job of teaching children anything—whether it's softball or geometry—we have a duty to expect the best from them, otherwise they'll never expect the best from themselves."

"My, what high idealism," she put in jokingly. "What about the Benton Cup? Surely each time Watch Point retains it there's an element of personal satisfaction."

"Ouch!" he said. "You certainly have a way of catching me at my most pompous, don't you? Well, I won't deny your charge, but the junior sailing program is more than a personal ego trip. The club has a reputation to uphold. And so do I, much as I may hate the fact sometimes."

"I don't imagine you hate it too often," she pressed. "In fact I'll bet you enjoy the attention your reputation brings you."

"It may surprise you to hear that I don't," he objected. "There is nothing gratifying in being merely the star attraction."

"Not even with women?" The words jumped out of her mouth before she could stop them.

James turned toward her. "Blunt, aren't you?"

"I—I'm sorry. I shouldn't have said that," she stammered. "Your personal affairs are no concern of mine."

"No, they're not," he replied stiffly. "Nor should you jump to conclusions. I suppose there's no point in trying to make you believe that the stories you've undoubtedly heard have little basis in fact. There are, however, some things I feel compelled to explain."

With his features in shadow Nicole could not read his expression. A breaker rushed in behind them and she hugged herself in her sweater. It had indeed grown cold.

"You're right that I've achieved a certain degree of

. . . notoriety," he went on. "But fame is an empty reward. There's no pleasure in being surrounded by fawning groupies, male *or* female."

"I didn't mean to suggest—"

"No, I'm sure you didn't," he interrupted. "Let me finish. Believe me, Nicole, it's far more satisfying to be understood and appreciated for what one truly is. That's one of the reasons I find you so refreshing."

"*Me!*" If anyone had misjudged him, it had been her, and the last thing she wanted was to draw his attention back to herself. She regretted now her unchecked impulse to tease him.

"Yes, you," James continued. If he was angry with her, at least it didn't show in his voice. "While I may find your behavior perplexing at times, one thing is certain: You haven't blindly accepted me at face value! Beyond that there's the fact that you're an alarmingly good little sailor."

"But surely you've met plenty of other women who are too," she protested, frightened by the direction of the conversation.

"I can see you haven't spent much time with the jet set. It's true that big ocean races draw crowds of beautiful women, but there are damn few that don't get seasick just standing on the dock. Still, that's not the only reason for my interest in you."

Panic clutched her. She was torn between a strange excitement and the desire to run. "I'm not sure . . . I mean, I don't think I understand."

"Don't you?" There was a sarcastic edge to his words. "A certain innocence is one of your charms, Nicole, but don't overdo it."

"I'm not!"

"No? Perhaps not, though I've already given you plenty

of hints. But if you need to have things spelled out, then so be it. The fact is that you're a very desirable woman. Too much so for your own good—or mine! When I found you lying in a heap by the roadside—"

A cry of surprise jumped from her lips. Had he known who she was even then?

"Yes, I knew," he said, reading her thoughts. "That morning was the first opportunity I had to call the club since returning from a trip to the Mideast. Steve explained the situation to me and I rushed down in the hope of catching you before you left."

So that was why he had come tearing down the road like a maniac. The irony of it struck her dimly.

He went on relentlessly. "You of course remember the condition I found you in. You looked so painfully vulnerable—a misjudgment, as I discovered shortly thereafter. But still, I couldn't help feeling some friendly angel had put you there for me to find. I knew instantly that I had to have you."

The directness of this confession took her breath away. Friendly angel! It had been some mischievous devil that brought them together, she thought ruefully. How could she possibly reply to this?

As it happened, words were unnecessary. He loomed over her like a thunderhead in the darkness. Like lightning his hand flashed toward her, his thick fingers tangling in her hair, snaring her.

Then his mouth was on hers, hungrily exploring. And to her dismay she felt herself responding. Her lips yielded to his eagerly, and her hands, moving under their own power, touched his hard, lean torso.

Now his arms circled her, drawing her suffocatingly close, and her own responded by reaching around his broad back. His kiss became more insistent, forcing her lips apart.

Inside her head a tiny core of sanity was crying for her to stop, but the power of his sensuous attack was too great. A hot fire roared into being inside her, sending sparks of desire shooting through her. She pressed herself to him almost desperately, her breasts crushed against the hard wall of his chest. Behind his back her fists held clumps of his shirt.

The sound of the breaking waves slowly retreated into nothingness. Her feet seemed to have left the ground. There was nothing in the universe except the two of them, locked together in the timeless grip of passion.

Afterward Nicole couldn't pinpoint what had broken the spell. The need to breathe, perhaps, but whatever the cause awareness suddenly came flooding back.

Letting her arms go limp, she jerked her mouth away from his and whimpered, "No . . . no . . . please . . ."

He did not hear her. Gently his lips began to tease the sensitive skin of her throat. With her head arched back, her nerves tingled. She was hovering on the edge of a great abyss, and in a moment she would go tumbling back down.

With a monumental effort of will she struggled out of his arms. Taking in huge gulps of the cool evening air, she turned and began to run.

It was miles back to town and very dark, but one thing was certain: She couldn't risk returning to him. His power over her was far too great.

Never before had she lost control of herself like that. Frightened by the vivid sensations still burning in her mind, she ran and ran. Finally, though, exhaustion overtook her and she slowed to a walk. The moon had come from behind a cloud and she saw that she had left the beach. She was on a road, but she could hardly make out its painted lines through the watery film on her eyes.

She was overwhelmed by a feeling of unreality. This was the kind of thing that happened to other people, not Nicole Tanner! She was stranded alone in the dark, far from anywhere. . . .

At that moment the Mercedes slid up next to her. She shrank back to the shoulder of the road as the passenger door popped open. In the weak glow of the interior light she could barely see James, but she heard his command clearly.

"Get in."

"No."

"Must I always force you into the car?" he said, his voice unaccountably gentle. "Get in, you can't walk all the way back. You don't know the way."

The simple truth of this statement struck her. There was no other choice. She climbed into the passenger seat and pulled the door closed, troubled by a feeling of relief as she did.

They drove back as they had come, in silence. Nicole was left alone with her thoughts, and she found she didn't like them.

She was attracted to him: it was silly to deny it. She had wanted him as much as he wanted her. Somehow he was able to suspend her reasoning faculties at will, and when he did, she inevitably submitted without a struggle.

Well, she would simply have to stay away from him as much as possible. But was that realistic? He had stated his intentions plainly enough, and besides, he would be supervising her closely.

A new thought struck her. He had convinced her that he had accepted her as sailing instructor on merit, but could it have been because he was attracted to her?

As her indignation grew she began to remember all the reasons she had to dislike him, all the tricks and traps he had worked on her. Grimly she gripped her armrest and considered the situation. If he was using his position to seduce her, that amounted to sexual harassment.

As they rolled to a stop in the Petersens' driveway, she reached quickly for the door handle, but he caught her free arm.

"There's no need to run away," he said gruffly. "Or are you afraid I'm going to attack you again?"

Nicole simply glared at him, barely containing her outrage. In contrast he appeared infuriatingly relaxed. A faint smile of amusement disturbed his perfectly sculpted lips.

"My company didn't seem to offend you a few minutes ago," he asserted.

Nicole balked at this attempt to intimidate her. "That was before you crossed the lines of propriety."

"Surely you're not as old-fashioned as that?" he mocked. "These days it's acceptable to kiss someone you're attracted to, you know."

"Not when she works for you—depends on you for her living!" she insisted.

"Ah, so that's it! The wicked boss pressing the helpless female for sexual favors, am I?" He released her arm and leaned back in his seat. "I think you'd better examine the situation before you call your lawyer. You haven't heard me threaten to fire you for failing to submit to my demands, have you? Furthermore, I've noticed a decided lack of resistance on your part."

With a sinking heart she realized he was right: There was no way she could prove she was being sexually harassed. Her cheeks burned with shame as she remembered the way she had pressed herself to him, returning his kiss.

"You may find me a demanding employer, Nicole," he went on deliberately, "but I'm not a tyrant. After all, there's no need to take advantage of our working relationship: I've only moved in where I found acquiescence to begin with."

She made a furious sound in her throat. The man's arrogance was absolutely beyond words!

"Not that that should worry you," he concluded lightly. "It's not illegal to fall in love, even with your boss."

"Fall in—" She choked in disbelief. "I'm not in love with you—and I never will be!"

"Don't be so sure," he returned, suddenly leaning close to her. Nicole shrank back, but somehow her arm refused to obey her command to open the door.

"Don't mistake me, Nicole," he said hoarsely, his voice barely above a whisper. "I'm a very determined man. The other night I observed that you lack experience. But you won't for long: I intend to give it to you—and I shall."

At last her limbs found their strength and she leaped out of the car and slammed the door closed with all her might. Quickly she ran up to the porch and darted inside the front door, looking back fearfully to see if he were following.

But he was not. His car was already in the road, its red taillights glowing menacingly as it roared away.

Fortunately the events of that evening were a distant, if distasteful, memory by the time the first sailing classes began the following week. James had not shown himself once during this interval, and Nicole had busily distracted herself with priming, painting, wet-sanding, and finally rigging the fleet of dinghies.

Then there had been two hectic days of registration. The students were assigned to one of three groups: beginners, intermediates, and the advanced class, who would concentrate on racing. The overall turnout was good, but to her dismay she found that only six of the forty-five youngsters qualified for the advanced class.

Only six possible defenders of the Benton Cup. From Steve she learned that unluckily a large group of outstanding young skippers had all passed the age limit together the year before. Crews could be recruited from the intermediate class this year, but nevertheless her hopes were still riding on precious few.

By alternating between shore classes and sailing sessions, she was able to spend two days out of three with each group. The beginners were by far the most fun; boisterous and eager to learn. And since they were also the youngest, they were the easiest to handle.

The intermediates, largely young teens, were more interested in each other than in paying attention, yet they were a bright group and learned quickly all the same. The advanced group was a problem, the "Sacred Six," as she called them privately.

By the first day of the second week of the program, these six difficult personalities had each become distinct. It was a blustery day, and because the high-speed gusts of wind would overpower the light dinghies, Nicole had opted for a shore class. They were seated on the floor of the main lounge, and she had spread her visual aids on the carpet. A cardboard arrow represented the direction of the wind, and a model sailboat sat precariously on a creased sheet of construction paper, representing a wave.

"Now, a 'broach' can cause you to capsize when you're going downwind," she was saying. "Can anyone explain how it happens? Alan?"

As usual, Alan Wentworth was looking elsewhere. Just like his father, he was a born bully. Because he was nearly seventeen and was somewhat more experienced than the others, he felt himself superior to the mundane routine of shore class.

"Yeah," he said, turning to her. Had he been listening, after all? "If you're stupid, you head upwind and the wind catches you sideways and knocks you on your butt."

Paul Bendix, Alan's cohort, snickered. By now Nicole was used to the fact that Alan talked this way mainly to shock her, so she kept her temper. She had spoken to his father the first time it happened, but the squat toad had snapped, "Never mind the kid's mouth. Just make sure he brings home some silver an' makes his old man proud." But he must have spoken to his son because Alan had curbed his tongue for several days afterward.

Now she decided it was time to take him down a notch. "No, I'm afraid you're wrong. Anyone else?"

Alan was taken aback by this unexpected rebuke. When no one else spoke, she succinctly explained the complex forces acting on a boat as it sailed downwind in a heavy breeze. For once they were all attentive as she told them how to counteract the dangers by shifting the crew's weight backward and steering a straight course downwind as the boat bucked over the waves.

Time to reinforce the lesson with questions. "Cindy, how would you steer the boat as you come off the back of a wave to avoid a broach?"

Shyly Cindy Bowman repeated what Nicole had told them. She was a pretty girl with long wavy golden-red hair. She was also a dead ringer for her twin brother, Todd, who was only slightly less reticent than his sister.

"Good," she said when Cindy had finished. "Now, Stu. Tell me why you pull the tiller toward you when you're being overtaken by a wave." Stewart Johnson and Patty Croft were the remaining two of the Sacred Six. They were both competent sailors, but the budding romance between them seemed to occupy most of their attention.

"Ummm . . . that's because . . ." Stu looked to Patty for the answer, but she only covered her mouth with her hand, stifling a giggle. Finally he blurted, "Oh, because the wave swings the bow into the wind, and pulling the tiller keeps the boat pointed down the wave instead of across it."

"Let's hope you don't have to stop to think about it when it actually happens!" came a deep, booming voice from across the room.

Nicole jumped several inches off the floor. There was no mistaking that voice. Her heart suddenly pounding, she swiveled around to face James. He was dressed casually in a Ralph Lauren polo shirt and a pair of faded jeans. With a shock she realized she had nearly forgotten how handsome he was.

It had been more than a week since their last encounter, and she had almost convinced herself that he had lost interest in her. She should have known better, she thought to herself as he came striding across to the group.

Towering over them, he commanded, "Okay, enough theory. Everybody into life vests and out to the boats."

There was a chorus of groans, but the Sacred Six quickly rose to their feet, responding automatically to the authority in his voice.

Nicole sprang to her feet as they shuffled out of the room. When they were out of earshot, she confronted him, fuming. "Don't you know it's gusting over fifteen knots out there?"

"Certainly," he replied. "What better conditions could you have for practicing today's lesson?"

"But we've barely covered the subject. This is a *shore* class," she protested.

94

"No one ever learned to sail by staying on shore," he countered sternly. Then, without giving her a chance to argue further, he strode out of the room.

Nicole was furious. His talent for getting on her nerves was remarkable, but for the moment there was no choice but to go along with him.

Outside it was sunny, despite the strong breeze. James had already started the small Boston Whaler she used to supervise on the water, and she climbed in next to him, glowering. It took only a few minutes for the Sacred Six to get their sails up, and soon they were tacking out into the chop beyond the breakwater.

James directed the exercises through a bullhorn. The little boats shot up and down the waves like roller-coaster cars, heeling far over under the force of the wind. Cindy and Todd Bowman were the lightest crew, and Nicole quickly noticed that they were having trouble keeping their boat upright.

"James, bring me over to them," she said, putting her hand on his arm. Touching him gave her a warm, breathless sensation, but he yanked back the throttle, and she had to grip the seat as the Whaler shot forward. He maneuvered them next to the floundering dinghy and Nicole leaped in nimbly and took the tiller from Todd.

"How're you doing?" she asked in an unruffled voice as James started off in another direction.

"N-n-not so good," said Cindy. Her teeth were chattering and she was clutching the jib sheet as if it were a lifeline, pulling it taut—exactly the wrong thing to do under the circumstances.

Patiently Nicole demonstrated how to keep the dinghy moving in a straight line, giving each of them turns at the tiller until she was sure they could handle the boat on their

95

own. When she was satisfied, she waved for James to pick her up.

She watched as the Whaler came skimming across the water, sending up bursts of spray each time it slapped a wave. His hair was blown back in the breeze, and his shirt rippled across the broad expanse of his chest.

An unexpected pang of longing hit her, but she angrily suppressed it. It was replaced by a feeling of resentment.

"They're terrified," she said after she had jumped back into the Whaler. "They shouldn't have been sent out in this wind."

"You were with them; how could they possibly have come to harm?" he said reasonably.

"That's not the point. They were simply afraid," she replied petulantly, brushing the hair out of her eyes.

"Yet, it's better to face your fears than to avoid them, am I right?"

Put in that way, it would seem foolish to disagree with him. For the remainder of the afternoon she maintained a hostile silence. At last the session was over, and once they had returned to the harbor, she retreated to the safety of her cubbyhole office on the third floor.

Flopping down in front of her battered wooden desk, she snapped on the small portable radio she had bought to keep herself company. Turning the volume low, she tuned in a classical station. A Ravel piano concerto was playing and the gentle music gradually soothed her frazzled nerves. She began flipping idly through a sailing magazine.

This calm interlude was short-lived, however. Responding to a knock on the door, she called, "Come in!"

James stood in the doorway, looking maddeningly neat and fresh with his hair just combed. Self-consciously she raked her fingers through her own short hair in a vain attempt to put it in order. The man had a positive knack for catching her looking her worst, she thought irritably.

Abandoning the task as hopeless, she propped her feet defensively on the edge of her desk. "Yes?" she asked with chilly brevity.

He did not answer right away, but instead flicked his eyes over her, taking in her long slender legs and the seductive curve of her bottom against the seat of the chair. His gaze traveled upward, resting briefly on the curve of her breasts beneath her plaid blouse, continuing up past the delicate line of her jaw, ending with her dark, flashing eyes.

Nicole flushed hotly under this examination but held his eyes with her own.

"I'd appreciate it if you wouldn't hide when we have business to discuss," he said finally.

"Who's hiding?" she snapped back, adding, "And what could there possibly be to *discuss,* anyway? You made it clear this afternoon that my opinion counts for nothing."

"If you'd stop being so rash for a minute, you might find out otherwise." His voice cracked like a whip. "But regardless of your mood there are times when we'll have to communicate, and at those times you'll simply have to put up with me, like it or not. Do I make myself clear?"

"Perfectly, O exalted one!" she replied defiantly.

A look of terrifying rage flashed across his face. He stepped into the room, slamming the door behind him. He seemed to fill the tiny office, crowding her deeper into the hollow of her chair.

"Sarcasm does not become you, Nicole," he said with awesome control. The sound of his voice speaking her name had an odd effect on her. If only once he could say it softly, tenderly . . . but of course she had done nothing to deserve kindness from him, she reminded herself.

"I'm sorry," she said quietly, genuinely regretting her immature anger.

His features relaxed and he leaned against the wall. "That's better. You know you're really very nice when you're behaving yourself."

He looked around her tiny office, taking in the bare walls, the porthole-size window with its partial view of the harbor, and the small bookcase jammed with sailing magazines.

"Are you comfortable here?" he asked.

"I could use another chair," she suggested, keenly aware that there was nowhere for him to sit. It was distracting to have him towering over her.

"Done," he promised. "Now, the reason I wanted to see you is that I have good news. I've set up a match against the Chattam Yacht Club's junior team. They'll be bringing six crews up here a week from next Wednesday."

"That's *good* news?" she gasped, incredulous. "That's just two weeks from now. They'll slaughter us!"

"Hey, have a little faith, will you?" he said, grinning. "We'll be ready for them."

Suddenly Nicole became suspicious. "*We . . . ?*"

"That's right," he confirmed. "I'll be assisting you for the next two weeks."

Assisting! He didn't know the meaning of the word. Directing, dictating, forcing—these were words that fit his style.

"But what about your plant?" she objected.

"I can spare a few hours a day," he explained. "My Mideast trip left us with a backlog of orders, so there's actually very little for me to do right now."

She didn't believe him for a minute. "But we can't possibly cover all the necessary ground in two weeks," she complained.

"That doesn't matter. We're in it for the experience. Remember, constant competition—"

"—is the best teacher. Yeah, I know, I know," she finished unhappily.

CHAPTER 5

As she rode home that evening her head was filled with scenarios for disaster. Her greatest worry, though, was the effect of being in daily contact with James. She wasn't sure she was up to that kind of emotional punishment. A single afternoon had left her drained.

As it turned out, though, his help proved to be entirely beneficial. In the shore classes his clear, well-organized lectures saved time and allowed them to accelerate the curriculum. On the water they worked as a team. James drove the Whaler, leaving Nicole free to go aboard the dinghies and give each of her students personal attention.

For their part the Sacred Six took up the challenge enthusiastically. Patty even took up a collection for Watch Point T-shirts, and when they were ready, the group proudly presented Nicole with her own snappy blue shirt with COACH printed on the back.

Five crew members were recruited from the intermediate class, and it was arranged for them to practice with the advanced skippers. Cindy and Todd Bowman insisted on staying together and Nicole agreed, requiring only that they take turns at the helm. Anything that would build up their confidence was welcome, she decided.

The two weeks flew by, and without being consciously aware of it, Nicole began to rely on James. He did not repeat his devastating advances, and for this reason she ceased to fear him.

The day of the match was sunny and mild with a weak southeasterly breeze. The Chattam team arrived, cocky and full of bravado. Nicole thought their confidence unwarranted, but when three races had been run and they returned to the club for lunch, she found that Chattam was ahead by a small but decisive margin.

The Watch Point team was spread out on the porch, gloomily devouring their brown-bag lunches. Nicole chewed her apple meditatively, reviewing the notes she had taken during the morning.

James had not yet turned up, which had left her feeling curiously abandoned. When he suddenly appeared at her side, though, her spirits magically improved.

"Fill me in on the situation," he ordered briskly.

Quickly Nicole reviewed the standings, wishing that his cutoff jeans and white sport shirt did not show off his deep tan so effectively.

"Looks like we'll have to pick up a few points," he said nonchalantly. "Let's get the group together and give them a pep talk."

Nicole leaped up and assembled the team. When they had settled in a circle, James addressed them in an easygoing voice. "Listen up! If we're going to beat these clowns, we're going to have to keep our heads screwed on straight and not fall apart during the last three races."

The group relaxed visibly, buoyed by his confidence. He continued, "Now, all three races were won this morning

101

by one of their skippers. Alan, do you have the guy spotted?

"Alan was obviously spoiling for a fight. "Yeah, I'd like to grind his—"

"Whoa! Heel, boy," James said quickly. "Getting mad isn't going to help. You won't beat him if you don't stay cool, right?"

"I guess," the boy admitted reluctantly.

"Okay, here's what I want you to do. Both you and Paul stay on this guy's tail. Turn the pressure on and he's bound to start making mistakes, got it?"

"All riiiight!" Alan exclaimed. Nicole watched with grudging admiration. Appealing to his need for revenge was something that would not have occurred to her.

"Good, now the rest of you: we've got a fluky southeasterly. Usually in this situation we get a wind shift late in the afternoon, so I want you to watch for it. Cindy, tell me what you're going to look for."

Cindy had been listening intently. Instantly she recalled, "Dark patches on the water. A line of clouds."

"Good girl. Stu, what do you always, *always,* do when you see a shift coming?"

"Tack toward it," Stu said.

Rapidly he went on to review the relevant lessons of the previous few weeks, and again Nicole had to acknowledge the wisdom of his approach. Associating the races with the familiar routines of their practice sessions made the situation far less formidable.

That afternoon Watch Point made a striking comeback. The leading Chattam sailor crumbled when faced with serious competition, and when the expected wind shift came, Cindy and Todd saw it long before anyone else. They tacked away from the fleet to take advantage of it and won the race.

Back at the club Nicole was ecstatic, but James only grunted noncommittally and said, "I expect we'll do better than that in the future."

And indeed as July crept along, Watch Point won a series of matches, éach time a little more easily than the last.

James had returned to work full-time, and Nicole was torn between an unconscious longing for his company and the uncertain hope that he had forgotten all about her. Her days became an agonizing jumble of long hours of teaching and idle evenings spent trying to keep her mind occupied.

It was a losing battle. A stack of paperbacks stood on her bedside table, all discarded before she had read fifty pages. Nor did television have its usual tranquilizing effect. Try as she might, she could not forget James's imperious warning. One day he would come to claim her, he had said, and she was not sure she would be able to resist him when he did.

But there was no word from him. Had he now dismissed her as a poor prospect for conquest? Oddly that thought left her feeling as unsettled as the dread suspicion that he was only biding his time. She felt like a soldier primed for a fight, yet dreading the coming battle.

It was Frank who finally broke the suspense. Nicole was sitting on the porch one evening, watching the sun sink below a roof on the opposite side of the street. The evening paper lay open on her lap, unread.

Frank ambled out the front door and plopped onto a chair next to her, his sleeves still rolled up above his elbows from his bout with the dinner dishes.

"Ahhhh . . ." he sighed as he settled in. "Just what I like. Lazy days in the sun and lazy evenings with nothing to do but digest dinner."

Nicole smiled at him. "Oh? I didn't know you were on vacation."

"Oh, I'm not," he explained, "but it feels like it, what with Boss Benton out of my hair."

Her face clouded. With James plotting further assaults on her emotional stability, no doubt he was neglecting his duties as slave driver at Benton Aircraft.

Frank's next words caught her by surprise, however. "Let me tell you, it's nice to have someone around who truly understands the burden under which I labor. I guess you must like being off the hook for a bit too, though, eh?"

Off the hook? If anything, she was slowly being reeled in. "What do you mean?" she asked.

"Sometimes that boat of his is a secret blessing," Frank rattled on. "It's the only thing one can count on to take him away from work. Now he's off in Los Angeles for the Transport, or some such thing."

The trans—? "Oh, do you mean the Trans*pac*?" she asked, realization dawning.

"Transpac. Yes, that's it," he confirmed.

So, James wasn't in Mannihasset Harbor at all! She sat up suddenly, which sent the newspaper cascading to the porch. As she bent over to collect the loose sheets, she considered Frank's news. The Transpac was a major ocean race—Los Angeles to Honolulu—so it stood to reason that James would enter *Warlord*.

With the paper reassembled, she turned back to Frank. "But I didn't know this! When did he leave?"

"Yesterday. And fancy this: he won't be back until the middle of next week. What luck!"

A great weight suddenly lifted from her shoulders. A whole week with James on the other side of the continent —halfway across another ocean, in fact! Perhaps this was only a temporary delay in their inevitable encounter, but at least she could go through the next few days safe in the knowledge that he wouldn't be pouncing on her without warning.

The next morning she practically floated across the footbridge to the club, for once wholeheartedly delighted to be going to work. It was early, so she stopped in the kitchen for coffee and found Peter there checking through a delivery of the vegetables he had shipped fresh daily from Boston.

He signed the deliveryman's invoice, then turned to greet her. "Ah, don't we look bright this morning. Someone has lifted the clouds that have been hanging over you lately, *non?* Come, come—you can't keep any secrets from me! It's James, isn't it?"

Nicole blushed, wishing her emotions weren't so easily read.

She was saved from replying, though, for Peter went on, "Ah, I am happy for you, but I must scold you as well. You have been making my job more difficult, you know."

"Me! How?" she asked, surprised.

Peter returned to the worktable where he had been folding tiny chunks of precooked lamb into pastry. "I am sure you know it is not easy to get ahold of our distinguished employer. For me there are always matters of club business to be discussed, *tu comprends.* Well, it used to be that I could expect to find him bringing some lovely woman for dinner every other evening! Then it was a simple matter to draw him aside, you see. *Et maintenant,* this summer, hmmm . . . no more fashion parade! Either he is hanging about *toujours,* making me a nervous wreck, or he does not appear for weeks. And I suspect I know who is to blame for this circumstance!"

Nicole flushed deeply, fully understanding him for the

first time. He thought they were romantically involved! How could she correct this gross misconception?

At just that moment, however, another deliveryman entered the kitchen, wheeling boxes of meat on a handcart. With Peter preoccupied she took her mug of coffee and the Boston paper the first deliveryman had left behind, and retreated to her office. She would set the record straight later. Right now she wanted only to relax, free from thoughts of James.

Setting the mug carefully on her desk, she flopped down in her chair. Somehow her drab little office seemed almost cheerful this morning. Bright lights streamed in from her tiny window, illuminating the two framed yachting prints that now hung on her wall. These and the additional armchair wedged into the corner had been requisitioned for her by—

But she was determined to erase James from her thoughts. She had half an hour before the first session and she was going to spend it all on herself. Not wishing to waste a minute, she turned her attention to the newspaper.

Her high spirits lasted only as far as the society pages. There, smack in the middle of a gossip column, was a small photograph of James. He was standing on a dock, entwined with the unmistakable figure of Sheilah Pritchard. The caption read PLAYBOY MILLIONAIRE SNAGGED?

Los Angeles, Cal. Boston's own Ted Turner, yachting superstar James E. Benton, was here today for the start of the Transpac L.A.–Honolulu ocean race. Spotted with him was Miss Sheilah Pritchard, the Massachusetts dairy heiress. Knowledgeable sources speculate that the unbeatable sailor may at last have met his match. Surf 'n' turf, Boston style?

* * *

With a disgusted cry Nicole flung the paper away from her. James and Sheilah Pritchard! The very idea made her feel sick.

She sat rigidly in her chair as a horrible realization came over her. She was jealous! Utterly, insanely jealous! How could that be? If anything, she should be rejoicing.

She felt her heart contract painfully. Could it be true that they were that deeply involved? Certainly Sheilah was not the type to be shy about grabbing what she wanted. Miserably Nicole remembered all the times she had repelled James's advances. Suddenly the thought of him kissing Sheilah, gathering her in the same strong arms she had felt around herself, seemed unbearable.

Her hand was trembling as she reached for her coffee. It had gone cold. Glancing at her watch, she discovered that she was late for her class, and she quickly made her way downstairs.

The day dragged on interminably. The sun was oppressively hot, but at last the dinghies were all tied to the dock, their sails folded and stowed in their locker, and she was making her way back across the footbridge to her bicycle.

"Hey, Nicky! Wait up!" Steve called from behind her.

She waited for him to catch up, uncertain of why he looked different until she realized that he had changed from his work clothes into a denim cowboy-cut shirt.

"Off early tonight?" she asked. Running the tender that ferried the members back and forth to their yachts often kept him until quite late.

"Yup. I finally got myself a part-time assistant," he explained, "and boy, am I ready for a night out! Would you like to take in a movie with me?"

Her initial impulse was to turn down this unexpected offer. All she really felt like doing was crawling into bed and sinking into oblivion. On second thought, however, she decided that a movie might be just the distraction she needed.

"What's playing?" she asked cautiously.

"In case you haven't noticed, there's only one choice in this town: the World Theater—not exactly a first-run showcase. I believe they're only just getting around to showing *Star Wars*. I've seen it before, but what the heck."

Nicole breathed a sigh of relief. At least it wasn't a heavy love story. Nor had she seen the movie before. "Sounds fine," she agreed.

They arranged a meeting time and Steve trotted off, looking pleased. After dinner and a long, cool shower Nicole changed into a pretty blue cotton sundress that left her shoulders and arms bare, and savagely brushed her short brown hair until it shone.

Normally she disliked science fiction, but *Star Wars* proved to be a delight. For two hours she was happily lost in its faraway galaxies, totally absorbed by the uneven fortunes and shining idealism of its heroes.

As they stepped from the air-conditioned dreamworld of the theater into the humid summer night, she felt thoroughly refreshed. Smiling at Steve, she thanked him for inviting her.

"Feel like a sundae?"

"Sure!"

They climbed into his ramshackle station wagon and drove to a busy ice cream stand outside of town. Everyone in Mannihasset Harbor under the age of eighteen seemed to be there. She saw a few of the Sacred Six, who snickered and elbowed each other in the ribs when they saw her and Steve standing together in line.

"What'll it be?" asked a white-clad matron with an enormous beehive hairdo when they reached the window.

"Ummm . . . a Banana Humdinger, please," she said.

108

Steve gave her an incredulous look. "Make that two," he ordered, adding, "If you're going to make yourself sick, I might as well join you."

She understood what he meant when the sundaes arrived in their plastic dishes. They were enormous, with two whole bananas sticking up from under mountains of ice cream, toppings, whipped cream, and nuts. The small plastic spoon tucked into the side of the dish looked woefully inadequate for its job.

Half an hour later, as they sat at a picnic bench to one side of the parking lot, Nicole's half-finished sundae had melted into a multicolored mass of liquid.

She set her spoon down and clutched her stomach in mock-agony. "Ugh. I think I'm gonna be sick!"

"Told ya." Steve laughed. He had finished his entire Humdinger long before and looked quite unaffected.

Despite the leaden feeling in her stomach, Nicole felt relaxed. It was easy to talk to Steve. There were no dangerous undercurrents to his remarks, though she did sense a nervousness behind his joking.

Her suspicions were confirmed when they arrived back at the Petersens' some time later. As she turned to thank him at the door, he awkwardly stepped up to kiss her.

Nicole hastily sidestepped his embrace. Then, before he had a chance to recover, she gave him a diplomatic peck on the cheek.

"Steve, thank you. I had a lovely time," she said sincerely.

"Yeah, me too," he agreed, abashed.

Seeing his disappointment, she offered, "Maybe we can get together another time? That is, if you ever get another evening off!"

"Sure, that'd be great," he said, looking less unhappy. "See you tomorrow."

"Good night."

As she crawled into bed a few minutes later, Nicole gingerly examined her feelings. It was unpleasant to have to shut Steve off, but it was impossible for her to see him as anything but a friend. Once it might have been different, but somehow James had permanently shattered her expectations as far as men were concerned.

James. What was he doing at that moment, she wondered? The pangs of jealousy she had felt that morning had diminished, but in their place was a dull longing. She wished now that she had not resisted him so stubbornly. Would she ever have another chance with him?

Oh, what did it matter! Anyone who could be swayed by Sheilah Pritchard's artificial charms deserved his unhappy fate. She was better off without him, Nicole told herself automatically, pulling her sheet up to her chin. Sleep, when it came at last, was black and dreamless.

By the end of the following week, though, James seemed a distant worry. He had been back for several days, she knew, after winning the Transpac by a healthy margin, but he had not yet reappeared at Watch Point.

It was just as well, she reflected. Her classes demanded her full attention. The Benton Cup was still five weeks away, but there was plenty of ground yet to be covered.

It was with a welcome sense of weariness, then, that she stopped in Steve's office late one afternoon and flopped into his spare chair.

"How's it going?" he asked, glancing up momentarily from his workbench.

"All right. What're you working on?"

"The carburetor from the tender," Steve answered, inserting his screwdriver with surgical precision. "Darn thing's been giving me trouble for weeks. I've ordered a

110

replacement, but Bensen's won't have it in for two weeks yet. Meanwhile I have to keep pulling it out and patching it up, which puts the tender out of service half the time."

"Are you getting any flak?" she asked, knowing how the Watch Point members disliked inconvenience.

"Not much. Things are pretty quiet during the week."

It was true. Virtually all of the club's one hundred or so yachts could be seen at their moorings that evening. But on a weekend the harbor would be practially deserted.

"Say," Steve said casually, his eyes fixed on the ailing carburetor, "how about that evening you promised me? I'm off again next Thursday."

"*Star Wars* again?" she teased.

"I don't think so. Even in a hick town like this they change the movie every once in while. How about it?"

"Okay," she agreed. Then suddenly she felt a prickling at the back of her neck. She twisted around in her chair.

Leaning coolly against the doorframe was James, an amused half smile on his face. He was dressed in a handsome gray summer-weight suit. His untrimmed hair was beginning to curl boyishly over his collar, and his face was an even deeper tan than before.

Nicole bristled inwardly. How long had he been standing there? And why was she suddenly embarrassed to have agreed to a date with Steve? The smirk on James's face irritated her unreasonably.

She suppressed her feelings, though, determined not to let him get under her skin. "Hello," she said brightly, forcing a smile.

He ignored her greeting and said in a stony voice, "If you're quite finished, I'd like to see you."

"But you see me this very moment," she countered lightly.

"I think you know what I mean."

111

She stayed where she was, staring at him with a look of happy defiance on her face. If he had anything to say, let him say it here!

When he realized her intention, a dark look passed over his features and he drew in a long, angry breath. Nicole glanced furtively at Steve for support, but he appeared to be absorbed in his carburetor.

"Very well," James said at last. "I assume you know that next Wednesday is Mid-Summer Madness."

"No, I didn't." The whole summer had been mad, it seemed to her. Why single out the middle?

"Do you know what that is?"

On reflection she remembered seeing Mid-Summer Madness listed as an event on the club's social calendar, but precisely what it was she didn't know. She shook her head.

James tucked his hands in his pockets and explained, "It's an annual tradition here: an evening race in small boats. It starts at six, which leaves several hours of daylight for the race itself. Afterward there's a clambake on Ely Island."

"Oh. So where does the 'madness' come in?" she asked.

"Ah! That refers to the rules . . . or should I say to the absence of rules."

You should know all about *that,* she thought to herself, biting her lip to maintain control.

"No rules at all? Anything goes?" she asked when her rebellious impulse had passed.

"Not exactly *anything,*" James said. "No outboard motors are permitted, for instance. Other than that, one must only start the race with everyone else and be certain that one's boat is decorated as imaginatively as possible. It is also traditional to circle each mark three times before proceeding to the next."

112

"Sounds like fun. I expect you want me to run the race."

"The social committee does that—it's their punishment for perpetrating this silliness," he said. A malicious gleam came into his eye. "No, I have other plans for you: you're going to crew for me."

"I'm . . . !" She stared at him in disbelief. "What if I refuse?"

"You can't. I'm ordering you—pulling rank."

"P-pulling rank!" she sputtered. He had to be kidding.

He *was* kidding. As she watched, the mischief in his eyes intensified. A grin tugged at the corners of his mouth as she continued to stare at him dumbfoundedly, and finally he tilted back his head and laughed. It was a pleasant, throaty sound that somehow defused the firecracker string of abuse she was about to hurl at him.

"Seriously," he said, "I need a crew, not least of all because I won't have time to decorate a boat in advance. And as you know, I always insist on the best: ergo, I'm asking you to sail with me.

"You needn't do it, of course," he added quickly, "but I'm hoping you won't sail against me instead. You might beat me hollow, and then I'd be disgraced in front of the entire club!"

Nicole was in a quandary. The last thing she wanted was to play Mr. Christian to his Captain Bligh, even for fun. Yet his appeal was so diplomatic that it would seem churlish to refuse.

There was no choice but to agree.

"Good. I've borrowed a Lightning for us, which I'll have sent down tomorrow. I'll leave the decorations up to you." With that, he turned and left.

Letting out her breath, Nicole found that her hands were locked to the sides of her chair like vices. "Oh, no!" she groaned. "What have I got myself into?"

"Don't worry," Steve said a little too cheerfully. "Mid-Summer Madness is a lot of fun."

"Oh, yeah! A barrel of laughs, I'm sure," she said, feeling worse than ever.

On the evening of the race her apprehensions had not diminished. Several times she had picked up the phone to call James and say that she couldn't crew for him, but she had been stopped each time by the realization that she had no excuse for backing out. Oddly the possibility of concocting a reason did not occur to her.

The mood was rowdy as the participants gathered at the club in their makeshift costumes. At least she didn't look out of place, she reflected.

Hearing that water fights were a traditional part of the race, she had dressed for action. She was wearing a very large man's white dress shirt over her bikini. Since it was missing most of its buttons, she had secured it around her waist with a long scarf. The tails had been shredded with a scissors, shipwreck-style, and she had tied her hair in place with a cloth headband.

At last, as the gaily decorated fleet was sailing out of the harbor, James arrived, smiling apologetically. Even in his ragged costume, he had managed to look stylish. He wore a denim shirt and a pair of faded jeans cut off below the knee. A red bandanna was knotted around his throat.

"Sorry I'm late." Running his eyes over her appreciatively, he said warmly, "You look quite appealing as a shipwrecked maiden, if I may say so!"

The knots in her stomach loosened a bit. "You're quite the handsome beachcomber yourself," she replied impulsively.

They made their way to the dock where the borrowed Lightning was waiting, its sails already hoisted. Not wishing to come off second best, Nicole had added a mock bowsprit and had lashed to the top of the mast a crow's nest fashioned from a small peach basket. Inside sat a rag doll with her stuffed hand sewn to her forehead to shade her button eyes as she scanned the horizon. The crowning touch, though, was a cardboard nameplate taped to the stern. It read: WARBABY.

Nicole held her breath, hoping the pun wouldn't anger him. To her relief he only laughed and said, "Excellent! Let's go."

The starting line was a model of chaos as several boats attempted to start backward, their crews screaming with laughter. James expertly steered them through the fleet, shouting joking threats to the boats they passed, and soon they were in the lead, tacking toward the first mark.

Nicole looked behind them. The fleet was a colorful sight, with hundreds of balloons and streamers flapping in the breeze. There was a great deal of laughter and good-natured shouting going on, she noticed.

As they approached the first mark there was only one other boat close to them, another Lightning. A wicked grin deepened the lines of James's face and he said, "Okay, mate. We're going to cause a little trouble."

They luffed their sails and fell back. James maneuvered them to within a few feet of the rival boat. Then, handing her the tiller, he shouted, "Stand by to repel boarders!"

With that, he nimbly leaped across to the deck of the other boat. The crew was in an uproar, shouting and filling buckets with water. In a flash, though, James had undone their halyard, and their mainsail came crashing down.

An instant later he was back aboard. Quickly Nicole trimmed the sails and they shot ahead, but not before their victims had lobbed several well-aimed buckets of water at them.

Soaked to the skin, but looking enormously pleased with himself, James took the tiller back from her. Nicole herself had been infected with his mischief and was beside herself with laughter.

"I—I say, Captain," she gasped, "is that legal?"

James chuckled. "I certainly hope not! Shocking behavior, don't you agree?"

Nicole only laughed some more by way of reply. In the excitement she had not noticed that she too was soaked, and the large shirt was now clinging wetly to her slender figure. Nor did she notice James discreetly examining her as she looked up, checking the trim of the sails.

Behind them the other Lightning had its sail back up, but they were now far ahead. They performed the required three revolutions around the mark and went speeding on toward the next.

As the noise of the fleet faded behind them, they were left alone with the familiar sounds of the wind in their ears and the waves slapping against the hollow wooden hull of their boat. Nicole removed her headband and shook her head, letting the warm breeze blow pleasantly through her hair.

She stole a look at James. His eyes were focused somewhere in the distance, narrowed to mere slits as he faced the wind.

Being confined in a small space with him was doing alarming things to her pulse rate. His wet clothes clearly outlined his hard, muscular frame, and his half-dry hair blew about his head in a way that made her long to run her fingers through it. A faint warning sounded in the back of her head, but she was enjoying these pleasant sensations too much to take note of it.

Certainly there was nothing threatening in James's childlike exuberance tonight. She considered the contrast

116

with his usual stern manner and decided that she liked the change.

They were working well together as a team too. Having grown used to his style of sailing, she could anticipate his orders, trimming and tacking in smooth harmony.

All too soon they were skimming across the finish line. The cannon aboard the committee boat fired to signal their victory and a chorus of horn blasts came from the spectator boats crowding the area. It was only a short sail to Ely Island, and a few minutes later they had pulled up the centerboard and were dragging the Lightning up onto the beach with the help of the club kitchen crew, who had been ferried out for the clambake.

They looked decidedly odd wearing their regulation whites on the beach, but oddest of all was Peter. Refusing to bow to convenience, he was supervising the preparations in his familiar, well-cut tuxedo.

One by one the other boats drew up and soon a noisy party was in progress. Plastic cups of beer were passed around and Nicole found herself a center of attention as interested parents grouped around her with congratulations and questions. In between answers she looked around for James, but he had disappeared into the crowd.

A tarpaulin was pulled back from a pit in the sand where net bags of clams, crabs, corn, and tiny potatoes had been steaming between hot rocks and mounds of wet kelp. Excusing herself, Nicole collected a plate of food and a cup of drawn butter, then sat down on a driftwood log to eat.

Fifteen minutes later a tiny mound of empty clamshells was piled in the sand in front of her. Wiping her mouth with a paper napkin, she sighed contentedly. The sun was down and the gathering quieted as bushels of clams were consumed with amazing rapidity. Someone had lit a bonfire and Nicole sat staring blankly into the leaping flames, feeling sleepy from all the food.

"Mind if I join you?" James's deep voice startled her, but she looked up at him and nodded silently, too tired to dredge up an appropriate remark.

He crouched down next to her, folding himself like an animal coming to rest. "Thank you, you did a marvelous job today," he said.

"You're welcome." How odd it was to hear those simple words coming from him. Unaccountably she felt a lonely ache inside.

"There you go, daydreaming again," James scolded her gently. "Mind if I ask what you're dreaming about?"

"Nothing at all, really. Sorry to disappoint you, but I think I'm just stuffed."

"Then you must walk it off." Uncoiling himself and rising to his full height, he held out his hand. "Come along, lazybones—no excuses!"

Nicole allowed him to help her up, her arm tingling from his touch. When she was standing, though, he dropped her hand. She felt curiously disappointed, though there was no reason why she should, she told herself.

Slowly he led her down the beach as it curved around the tiny island. As if on cue the moon had come up above the mainland, sending a bright beam of light across the water. For some reason it seemed like a shimmering bridge —leading to an impossible, fairy-tale life, she decided unromantically.

They walked in silence for a few minutes, James with his hands in his pockets and his eyes on his feet, Nicole trying to get a grip on the confused emotions swirling around inside her.

At last he broke the uncomfortable silence. "You don't like me very much, do you?" he asked.

Nicole was completely taken aback. How could she answer this? A few weeks ago she might have known how she felt, but now she wasn't sure. Instead of answering, she asked a question of her own.

"Why must you win at everything you do? Doesn't that take the pleasure out of life?"

Immediately she regretted this criticism, but James did not seem to mind. He answered, "To take your questions in reverse order: yes, sometimes being competitive does take the pleasure out of life. But sometimes it's the only thing that makes life at all interesting. It depends on the circumstances. As for the first question—why I'm competitive in the first place—there's no easy answer for that, I'm afraid."

"I'm sorry, I shouldn't have asked."

"No, no. You deserve an answer, Nicole. I'm just not sure I can give you one that you'll understand."

He paused, apparently searching for words, and she sensed that he was not accustomed to talking about himself.

"It has a great deal to do with my childhood, I suppose," he said finally. "My mother died when I was very small."

"So did mine," Nicole put in, though she wasn't sure why.

"Did she?" He sounded genuinely surprised. "But you're so—"

Different than me? What had he been about to say? she wondered.

He chose to leave the thought incomplete, however. He stopped to throw a stone into the ocean. It curved far out over the water, and she heard, rather than saw, its distant splash.

He continued, "Anyway, I was raised by my father, a

cold man who was only concerned that I learn the value of hard work. Although we were quite well off, I was never given an allowance. I earned my pocket money working around our estate. Felling trees—*hard* work." He snorted. "Our estate has miles and miles of those broken-down New England stone walls. I would rebuild them—ten cents for ten feet."

Nicole gasped. "That means you'd have to rebuild a hundred feet just to earn a dollar!"

"Slave wages, yes," he agreed. "But I must hand it to the old man. To this day I think of the value of a dollar as the sweat and aching muscles that goes into a hundred feet of wall. I earn a lot of money now, but I work for it, you can be sure."

An idea flashed into her head. "And you still rebuild those walls yourself, don't you?"

He looked sideways at her. "How did you know that?" he asked curiously.

Nicole didn't reply. So, that was how he managed to keep himself in such good shape!

After a moment he continued his reminiscences. "My father didn't even pay for my education. I worked on the line at the plant during the summers, and even at school I always had part-time jobs—waxing floors, dishwashing."

This was completely contrary to her image of him as a spoiled rich kid, born to wealth and authority. He stopped to throw another stone, as if casting away this bitter memory.

"But Frank told me you even did graduate work. That must have been expensive."

"Yes, a Ph.D. in aeronautical engineering is not cheap. I won scholarships, but I paid for most of it with veterans' benefits."

"You were in the service?" she asked, surprised. She couldn't imagine him taking orders from anybody.

"Four years in the Air Force," he answered with unexpected bitterness.

"Is that where you learned to fly?"

"No, I had my pilot's license by the time I was sixteen."

The number of things he had done in his life boggled her. "How old are you, anyway?"

"Thirty-four."

Thirty-four. She considered the difference in their ages. When he had been in college, she was still calling boys' names across the playground.

Some further calculations told her that he had probably also flown in Vietnam. Did that have something to do with his bitterness a moment ago? It might also explain why his company no longer made military aircraft, she realized.

By this time they were out of sight of the rest of the group. The sand had given way to a rock beach, and they were prevented from speaking for a few minutes as they jumped from one large stone to another, hopscotch fashion.

"Hey, try this!" he challenged her. With acrobatic ease, surprising for someone his size, he skipped lightly across a particularly difficult combination of stones, ending on top of a large boulder.

Swiftly Nicole imitated his moves, her feet dancing the complicated rhythm as if they had a mind of their own. She leaped up next to him with a triumphant "Ha!"

For an instant they were only inches apart. Nicole froze, holding her breath, realizing suddenly that she desperately wanted him to take her in his arms.

For a moment it seemed as if he would. His hawk eyes burned, but then the fire in them died. She thought a look

121

of sadness swept across his features and vanished, but it might have been a trick of the darkness.

"Not bad," he said lightly, "but for how long would you be willing to keep up with me?" Without waiting for an answer to this mysterious question, he stepped off the boulder and continued down the beach.

In a moment of shocking clarity of the sort that comes only once or twice in a lifetime, Nicole understood that this was a turning point.

She knew she should not follow him. She should turn around and go back to the others—back to a life safe in its predictability. How could she ever hope to tangle with so complicated a man and emerge intact?

But some deeper need—a need for a higher fulfillment, perhaps—took hold of her at that moment and she nimbly leaped off the boulder and hurried after him.

She caught up with him on the sandy beach on the far side of the island. They walked together in silence for a minute. Spread before them was the vast empty expanse of the Atlantic Ocean, luminescent in the moonlight. For the first time the sight made her feel isolated and afraid.

When James began speaking again, his voice was rigid with suppressed emotion. "It's true that I often see life as a series of contests. Yet in a contest one must always be certain of one's goal—absolutely certain that one wants to win the prize. If there is the least doubt, you will lose. Do you understand?"

"I—I think so."

"Do you? I wonder." He stopped walking and turned to her. "Nicole, I think you are waging a needless contest with your heart. Have you considered this? Have you weighed those things you stand to win or lose?"

Her head was spinning. "I don't know what you mean."

"Yes, you do. Please, Nicole! For once don't be stub-

122

born just out of habit. Listen to your heart. You're in love with me."

No! No! The word repeated itself for a moment, then went whirling away in the vortex of doubt. She wanted to hate him, to thrust him away, but now she had seen new sides of him: high-spirited, charming, courageously self-aware. He was complex and sensitive—a man who could fascinate her for a lifetime. Damn him!

Then, magically, she was in his arms and all reason was abandoned. The treachery of words gave way to the pure, sweet language of desire.

His mouth on hers was hungry, demanding, and her own supplied all that he asked. Their tongues mingled in a wet, sensual dialogue for what seemed an eternity. James gathered her more closely in his powerful arms. Her body became pliant, molding itself to his hard contours: the fire he had started seemed to have melted her very bones.

Slowly his hands began tracing circles up and down her back. The pleasure was exquisite, and a soft groan came from deep in her throat. She tore her mouth away from his and instantly he began to kiss the soft flesh of her neck. With her head arched back, her eyes squeezed shut, Nicole felt the world begin to spin. But gradually the dizzy sensation diminished, and it seemed as if the two of them were floating in space.

She had no idea how much time had passed when she finally became aware that he was whispering her name, his mouth somewhere near her ear.

"Nicole," he groaned softly. His hands left their places behind her back and traveled up to cradle her head tenderly, as if it were a fragile piece of crystal. His lips were only an inch from hers. "Darling, say you love me."

She could not trust herself to form the words. Instead she nodded her head slowly.

His passion exploded again, sending her senses rocketing back into some outer envelope of the atmosphere. As his mouth explored hers one of his hands pulled away the scarf around her waist and flipped her shirt apart. As his hands slid around the bare skin of her back, her body began to tremble.

Then he brushed the shirt off her shoulders, and in an instant he had unhooked the flimsy top of her bikini and cast it away. The delicious feel of her skin exposed to the air overpowered her, stifling the protests she knew she should have made.

With one hand locked behind her, his other explored the length of her back, her bare shoulder, and moved down to cup the swell of her breast. The intimacy of this movement inflamed her beyond anything in her experience. There was no going back now, she knew. She wanted him to possess her totally.

But it was not to be. At that moment the sound of approaching voices shattered their warm cocoon. With a shock Nicole was wrenched back into cold reality.

Panic-stricken, she broke from his arms. The voices were growing closer. There was a mumbled remark from a man, followed by a distinctive silvery laugh: Sheilah Pritchard!

Desperately Nicole searched for her missing clothes. She found her shirt lying a few feet away and snatched it up, but the top of her bikini was nowhere to be found. Choking back a sob of humiliation, she fell to her knees and began groping in the sand.

"Jiiiimmy!" Sheilah's wavering voice disintegrated into a horrible laugh.

"There he is," said a male voice.

"Damn, damn, damn!" she heard James muttering.

The group was almost upon them. There was no time

to look further for her bikini top. Quickly Nicole rose and pulled on her shirt, folding it closed in front of her as Sheilah stumbled up, half-supported on either side by a man. How much had they been able to see in the darkness? she wondered.

"There you are you, you rat!" She had obviously had a good deal to drink. Seeing Nicole, she added, "Soooo! Chasing after the help now, are we?"

James stood with his arms folded, his face impassive. "Hello, Sheilah," he said coolly.

Sheilah ignored him, her attention taken up with Nicole. Her eyes narrowed. "Listen, you. This is more man than you know how to handle. Why don't you run on home, hmmm?"

Nicole felt as if she had been slapped in the face. She looked at James, silently pleading with him to help.

But his eyes were fixed on Sheilah. "You can take your claws in," he told her in a studiously matter-of-fact tone. "Miss Tanner and I are only settling a difference of opinion."

The blood drained from Nicole's face. She felt as if she had been slapped again. *Miss Tanner* . . . was that all she was?

Sheilah was not satisfied with this victory, however. "Just s-s-settling a difference of opinion, are you?"

Shaking off her two escorts, she grabbed a piece of cloth that was lying under her foot and dangled it from her forefinger. It was the missing bikini top.

"And what do you call this?" she said. "A peace offering?"

CHAPTER 6

Afterward Nicole's memory of the scene that followed was mercifully hazy, though certain details remained vividly clear: Sheilah taunting as she scornfully waved the bikini top like a captured flag; James snatching it and tossing it to her with a growled "Get dressed."

Somehow the group had made its way back to the other side of the island. Nicole remembered only her riotously conflicting feelings of frustration, relief, and humiliation. That, and Sheilah hanging possessively on James's arm, forcing him to support her.

With the bonfire reduced to a heap of glowing embers, the party was breaking up. James had disappeared with Sheilah on her mammoth cabin cruiser, leaving Nicole to find an obliging motorboat owner to tow the Lightning back to the club.

The following day found her alone in the Whaler, drifting aimlessly while the Sacred Six sailed their practice races. In the long hot intervals, as she waited for them to finish, she tried to put her chaotic emotions into a logical perspective.

Fact one: It was no longer possible to ignore the reality that she had been avoiding for so long—she was hopelessly in love with James.

In love with James. She turned the idea over in her head coldly, handling it as if it were an oddly shaped artifact from some distant civilization. Once she had thought that love would be a safe, comfortable emotion, a rare gift bestowed once in a lifetime. But James had ruined that ideal beyond recovery. Love, she had discovered, was an all-too-explosive disorganization of the mind and senses.

Loving James was the most profound experience of her life, yet it had led only to hurt and humiliation: that was fact two. Was he merely careless with his affections, or was he a master of illusion? His seduction had certainly been breathtakingly real. She had readily believed that his feelings for her were as genuine as hers for him.

Probably James cared no more for women than for a chance wind shift. If one happened along conveniently, he would take advantage of it. Her cheeks burned as she remembered how casually he had abandoned her for Sheilah the night before. Well, if she represented the kind of "experience" he wanted in a woman, then let her have him!

The overhead sun was oppressively hot. Nicole slumped down and pulled her baseball cap low over her eyes. Relentlessly she forced her thoughts onward.

The undeniable truth was that James was a ruthless game player. He had told her so himself: once he fixed a goal in his mind, he didn't stop until he had achieved it. All that mattered to him was the abstract ideal of winning.

No, there could never be any hope that he would grow to love her in the way she needed. An enduring respect,

127

a concern for someone that transcended selfish needs—these human qualities were beyond his capability, she decided.

And yet . . . and yet . . . she could not shake the feeling that there was some deeper aspect to the man, deeper needs that he yearned to fulfill. Perhaps in demanding so much from himself and others he was reaching for a higher goal, something beyond the grasp of other mortals. Should she abandon her petty fears and trust herself to his peculiar genius?

No! Angrily she rejected this idea. It was an illusion. James's needs were purely animal. And like the great predators of the jungle, he survived by preying on the easiest game. Last night had been the perfect example.

Which led her to fact three: There was only one way in which she could hope to survive in this jungle of emotions. She must avoid the hunter, no matter how much it cost her. Thank goodness she would be spending the evening with Steve!

A distant rumbling interrupted her thoughts. Sitting up, she saw a line of thunderheads off to the south. Picking up her whistle, she sounded three long blasts to signal the crews to abandon the race.

They made it back to the harbor with only minutes to spare. The sky had darkened quickly, and no sooner had the sails been folded and stowed than it let loose a torrent of rain.

It was still pouring that evening as Nicole waited on the Petersens' porch for Steve to arrive. She had thrown a yellow poncho over her jeans and plaid flannel shirt. As a further concession to the weather, her habitual sandals had been replaced by sneakers. Steve was taking her to what he promised was the best burger joint in Massachusetts, and her stomach was growling in anticipation.

At last a pair of headlights pulled into the driveway. Without waiting, Nicole dashed down the steps and went leaping across several puddles. With water streaming off her, she was laughing as she yanked open the passenger door. She dropped into the seat saying, "Whew! I couldn't make you get out of the car in *that*!"

"How considerate," purred a deep voice next to her.

James! With a shock of dismay she twisted sideways and saw the familiar expression of faint amusement on his face. Looking around, she recognized the Mercedes—the doom car.

"Oh, no, you don't!" she exclaimed angrily. "I'm afraid I have other plans for the evening!"

She reached for the door handle, but James had already jammed the car into reverse and was backing down the driveway.

"Hey, stop! Let me out!"

"In due course," he said, looking backward over his shoulder.

Something had to be done. As the car started moving forward down the street, she opened her door, letting in a shower of water.

"Damn it, shut that door!" he barked. "Do you want to get killed?"

"I want you to stop the car and let me out," she insisted.

He responded by pressing down on the accelerator. Wet pavement flashed past and she could hear the loud hiss of the tires. It would be impossible to jump out without injuring herself. Reluctantly she pulled the door shut.

"Just what do you think you're doing? I have a date, and I intend to keep it. If there's any business to be discussed, it can wait until tomorrow. I'm off duty!" She tried to sound firm, but the tremor in her voice was clearly audible.

"If you'll get a grip on yourself, I'll explain. Your date has been canceled," he announced.

"You can't do that!" she spat furiously.

"My dear, I had nothing to do with it. The tender broke down completely late this afternoon and Steve is staying late to fix it. I happened to be at the club, so I offered to pass along his apologies."

"A telephone call from either of you would have been sufficient. It was hardly necessary to kidnap me."

"You aren't being kidnapped," he replied with infuriating sangfroid. "I'm only going to supply the evening out you were already expecting. And under the circumstances you can hardly expect me to believe you have anything else to do."

"What did you have in mind? Dinner for two at the Chamber of Horrors?" she snapped.

He studiously ignored her sarcasm. "Someone at the plant gave me two lobsters today, and they must be eaten while they're fresh. And don't tell me you don't like lobster, either. Peter tells me otherwise."

Damn his arrogance! She fumed silently. Perhaps it was just as well, she decided. A confrontation was inevitable, so the sooner it was out of the way the better.

They drove northward out of town in chilly silence. Nicole did not look at him once. She felt sick with fury. It would be more pleasant to have dinner with the devil himself, she reflected. He, at least, could be counted on to be polite.

After almost half an hour James turned the car onto a private road. They followed several twists and turns, and after a minute vast green lawns came into view. Some of

Nicole's anger was supplanted by curiosity as she looked around.

There were stables and a barn off to her right, and they passed banks of carefully tended flowers. Indeed, everything in sight was immaculately kept.

"Where are we?"

"I live here," James answered simply.

Nicole was impressed but was determined not to show it. The road curved up to a large mock-Tudor mansion. Its two-story white facade—with its crisscross pattern of exposed beams—was beautiful, and yet somehow the building looked imposing rather than cozy.

James parked the car beneath a sheltered entranceway. Once inside, he hung her poncho in a hall closet and led her into the living room, pausing to flip on a bank of light switches.

Nicole gasped involuntarily. The room was vast. A giant fireplace dominated the far wall, and a wide bay window overlooked the lawns. Comfortable-looking sofas and chairs in successive pastel shades were grouped together on carpeted islands around the room, and a tasteful selection of contemporary paintings hung on the walls.

It was indisputably beautiful, yet there was still something impersonal about it. It was *too* perfect—too clean of the debris of daily life, like something from a Sunday magazine. Probably an interior decorator had designed it, she decided.

James gestured toward a sofa and told her to sit down, then crossed to an artfully disguised liquor cabinet.

"Drink?"

For a moment Nicole considered refusing, but decided it would be pointless to be objectionable on minor issues. "Dubonnet, if you have it."

He poured her drink and a Scotch for himself. Handing

it to her, he said, "Now, I hope you won't mind if I go change out of this suit."

"Not at all," she answered without interest, thinking, *Take an hour. No rush.*

If her offhand manner had any effect on him, he didn't show it. He pointed to another cabinet and said, "There's a stereo there. Put on a record, if you'd care to." With that, he strode out of the room, carrying his drink.

Nicole let out her breath and set down her drink, grateful for a break in the tension. Perhaps some music would help settle her jittery nerves after all.

She crossed to the stereo, wondering what sort of record collection he would have. Classical, no doubt—all the gloomy modern composers.

As she surveyed the shelves of records, though, she was surprised to find a wide-ranging collection of jazz and rock groups. With albums by the B-52's, Roxy Music, and Robert Fripp it was astonishingly up-to-date. Not even her college friends had been that hip!

Finally she selected the jazz singer Al Jarreau. When the record was on, she returned to the sofa. The soft syncopation of the music lulled her, and she put her head back and closed her eyes.

"You haven't touched your drink."

At the sound of his voice her eyes snapped open. He was standing over her, looking relaxed and comfortable in jeans and a white Irish fisherman's sweater. A fresh drink was in his hand. How had he fixed it without being heard?

"Why don't you bring that into the kitchen with you? You can keep me company while I fix dinner," he suggested.

Again Nicole considered refusing but decided against it. Seeing the living room had made her curious about the rest of the house.

The kitchen was large and well equipped, obviously designed for large-scale entertaining. A square butcher block table occupied the center of the room and from the rack above it hung an array of pots, pans, and fish poachers.

James set to work, filling a large pot with water and placing it on a burner. He set a brown paper bag on the worktable and pulled two large lobsters from it. They immediately started to skitter away, but he deftly caught them in either hand and deposited them in the sink. Moving to the refrigerator, he extracted an assortment of salad greens and a stick of butter, which he put in a saucepan and set on the stove.

Nicole was acutely aware of the uncomfortable silence between them. At last, simply to relieve the tension, she asked, "Surely you don't keep this place up all by yourself?"

James gratefully took up this neutral subject. "No, a maid comes in several times a week. I also have a grounds-keeper who lives in an apartment over the stables."

He was standing at the worktable with his sleeves pushed up to his elbows, chopping a hard-boiled egg. Suddenly this struck her as odd. "Don't you have a cook too?"

"No. When I'm not eating out, I generally fix something simple for myself. On those occasions when I'm forced to entertain I have a caterer come in," he explained, gesturing at the hanging utensils.

She doubted whether he had to be "forced" to entertain but held her tongue. He continued working with practiced ease, quartering a lemon with two swift strokes.

Despite herself, she was feeling guilty about letting him do all the work. Now that the shock of the evening's turn of events had worn off, she began to regret being recalci-

133

trant. Putting up a fight was going to get her nowhere; invariably he overpowered her.

"Shall I set the table?" she offered.

"Yes, that would be a help. Dishes are there, and the table's through there," he said. Indicating a pair of sliding glass doors, he added, "Watch your step."

Nicole gathered plates and silverware and pulled aside one of the doors. She stepped down into the next room, startled by what she saw. She was in a glassed-in patio.

No, on second thought it was more like a greenhouse, she decided. Tall tropical plants stood all around, and a variety of flowering vines hung from the curved steel framework overhead. Rain spotted the broad expanse of glass, pattering pleasantly.

Making her way in the half darkness, she moved further into the room and found a round marble table surrounded by a half dozen wicker chairs. She switched on an industrial-shade lamp hanging over it, pleased with the warm oasis it created.

It took only a few minutes to set two adjacent places. Surveying the table when she had finished, she thought better of it and moved one of the settings farther around, leaving an extra chair as a buffer zone.

A moment later James came in carrying a bowl of salad and a tray of dressings, lemon wedges, and melted butter. "Very nice," he said noncommittally as he examined the table.

Nicole sat down. He was back a minute later with the two steaming bright red lobsters on a platter and an open bottle of wine.

He set these on the table, and as he settled into his chair Nicole sneaked a look at the wine label. Pouilly Fumé. She frowned. French, presumably, though she had never heard of it. No doubt he liked his wines as exotic as his women.

He poured some of the pale straw-colored liquid into each glass. Holding his up, he said seriously, "Here's to lobster."

"Yeah, big and tough on the outside, but not much meat inside," she replied wickedly, touching the rim of his glass with hers.

James was unruffled by this remark and calmly proceeded to work on his lobster, expertly twisting off a claw. Nicole tasted the wine. It was deliciously crisp—not at all unpleasant.

Suddenly she realized she was still very hungry. She attacked her lobster voraciously, pulling off its tail and extracting the meat in one large piece.

"I see you've had some practice at this," James commented.

"Some," she answered shortly. For the moment she was more interested in eating than in verbal swordplay. Systematically she cut the tail meat into neat rounds and sprinkled them liberally with lemon and butter. Popping them into her mouth, she savored their sweet flavor.

James had no trouble keeping up with her. After their initial surge of hunger had passed, he paused to sip his wine. Cautiously he asked her about her progress with the Sacred Six.

In between mouthfuls Nicole dutifully filled him in, and gradually the conversation turned to sailing in general.

"Tell me about your trip to the Mideast," she asked during a lull in the talk.

"All right," James agreed and launched into an account of his travels. He was a surprisingly good observer of culture and customs, and quite unconsciously Nicole became absorbed in his colorful stories of the crowded bazaars of Tunis and the elaborate protocol of official Cairo.

She stopped him with occasional questions, but for the most part his steady stream of anecdotes carried them through the remainder of their dinner. Nicole had long since finished eating and was sipping her third glass of wine by the time he concluded a particularly funny story about a distraught Egyptian officer and his missing pet cobra.

"So the ambassador's wife, who was remarkably collected under the circumstances, said, 'My dear Colonel Khalad, your snake is worth far more than that! It has just swallowed my ruby!' "

Nicole burst out laughing. "Did she get her ruby back?"

"Yes, but the poor snake was dispatched to the arms of Allah, I'm afraid. The unhappy colonel swore he would keep a dog from then on," James said. "Now, are you ready for some dessert?"

"Oh, you're kidding. I'm stuffed," she replied. Her full stomach ached even more from laughing.

"Ah, but I have something you won't be able to resist," he promised mysteriously. "Help me carry these dishes in."

Back in the kitchen Nicole carefully scraped and stacked the dirty dishes while James cradled a copper bowl, whipping cream with a wire whisk. Feeling sleepily satisfied from the food, she let her imagination wander.

There was something agreeably warm and cozy about the simple chores they were performing. The complacent domesticity of marriage had never appealed to her, but now it occurred to her that being married to James would be anything but dull. How nice it was to be surprised with lobster and wine on a rainy summer night.

She stopped herself. Marriage! What was she thinking?

136

Gratefully she recognized the delicious smell of brewing coffee. Just what she needed: the wine had evidently fogged her brain!

She carried a tray with the coffee service into the living room. After setting it on a low table, she went to the stereo. Some loud music would help to keep her alert.

Searching the rock 'n' roll end of the shelf, she pulled out what appeared to be an appropriate record. When she had put it on the turntable and gently lowered the tone arm, she returned to the sofa and poured herself coffee.

The music that came out of the speakers a moment later was not what she expected. It wasn't hard rock at all, but soothing waves of slow, mystical electronic sound. It was entirely pleasant, but too relaxing.

Before she could get up to change it, however, James came in carrying two tall dessert glasses with long spoons tucked into them. He set one of these in front of her.

"R-raspberries," she choked.

"Yes, fresh picked. There's a whole patch of them out back," James explained, unaware of the fruit's unhappy associations.

Nicole studied her dessert with a sinking heart. The bright red berries were topped with a dollop of rich-looking whipped cream. Ordinarily she would have gobbled up this treat, but now it only reminded her of their first stormy encounter. Suddenly without appetite, she toyed with her spoon for a moment, then set it down.

James had placed himself a safe distance from her on the sofa. Pouring himself coffee, he said, "Dessert doesn't tempt you?"

Nicole kept her eyes on the floor. "Why did you bring me here tonight?" she asked.

The question brought him up short. She was expecting

a light rejoinder, but he answered seriously. "I would have thought that evident: to finish what we began last night."

With a soft cry of alarm she began to rise from her seat.

"Take it easy," James commanded. "I'm not going to attack you. I've conducted myself with superhuman restraint so far this evening, and I won't spoil it now. I only meant that we should finish our conversation. I intend to resolve whatever is keeping us from each other, which I'm unlikely to do if I use force."

Nicole sank back down with an air of resignation. She didn't see what he could possibly say that would right the wrongs he had done her.

"Okay, so talk," she said bitterly.

James exploded. "You are the most exasperating woman I have ever known! One minute I think I've succeeded in coaxing you out of your armed fortress and the next I find you've retreated farther from me than before. What have I said to offend you? Please, tell me!"

"But don't you see, it isn't that!" She had intended to sound harsh, but her tone was almost pleading. "You've never said anything that didn't make perfect sense, and in a way that's the problem. Words are so convincing, but they can never substitute for actions. . . ."

She trailed away, defeated by the enormity of what she was trying to express.

James studied her for an unbearably long minute, his face impassive. Then he said tightly, "Obviously you find something unworthy in my behavior, but I'm at a loss to know what."

"Last night—"

"Ah, is that it!" He seemed to relax at this revelation. Sinking back in the corner of the sofa, he spread his arms to either side and laughed briefly with an air of relief that

138

was not entirely convincing. Nicole remained huddled in her place, watching him with a hostile expression.

"Last night was one of the most frustrating of my life!" he explained. "That regrettable interruption made me as furious as I've ever been."

Nicole was not to be won with this weak explanation. "You left with that . . . with *her,* after all!"

"My dear, what choice did I have? Sheilah was shamelessly drunk, in case you failed to notice. It would have been quite inconsiderate of me to allow her to continue disgracing herself as she did. The only option was to remove her from the scene, and believe me, nothing has ever given me greater pleasure."

"I'll bet," she replied automatically.

His face tightened. Stiffly he said, "You don't believe my motives were innocent? Would it help if I were to swear to you that I did nothing more than bring her home—then come back to search for you? I was desperately hoping you would be waiting for me; vainly, as it turned out."

Nicole didn't answer. She did not doubt the honesty of this account, but even if it was true, it did not change his essential nature. In a larger sense her expectations were simply too far from the reality he offered.

When she failed to respond, he angrily left his seat and crossed to the liquor cabinet. He was back a moment later, swirling brandy in a snifter. He took a large swallow before turning his attention back to her.

"Nicole, I don't know what it is I must do to redeem myself in your eyes. You say you don't trust words, and justifiably so. Too often in life we misapprehend each other's intentions and break our promises. But if my words can't convince you, what else can I do? I've tried to demonstrate my feelings more directly, but every time I touch you, you run away."

The mixture of frustration and sadness in this speech touched her unexpectedly. She forced herself to look away from him.

"What is it I must do, Nicole?" he repeated. "Last night . . . last night you said you loved me."

She hadn't, she remembered, but she had wanted to, and now she wanted to console him, to confess the true depths of her feelings. Yet she could not; past disappointments still weighed too heavily.

"Last night I accused you of being competitive," she said in a small voice. "You explained why, but explanations don't change the way you are. To you life is a game . . . and I'm just another sort of trophy to be won, don't you see?"

He sat up suddenly. "My God, how can you say that? Do you have any idea what a rare creature you are in my experience? I couldn't 'win' you if I tried! Not once have you ever accepted a fatuous compliment from me; you're much too intelligent for that. Yet never have my compliments been more sincere in intention. There are times when I positively ache with tenderness for you."

It took all the willpower she had to keep from throwing herself into his arms at this. "Pretty words," she said, "but they're just words. Don't you see I need more than that?"

"Yes . . . all too well! But for some reason you won't let me give it to you."

"No, you don't understand what I mean!" she cried. "It's not just sex. I could go to anyone for that, I suppose."

"If you do," he growled, "I think I would go insane with rage."

"It would serve you right," she taunted, "but it would

still be your vanity that was offended, not your heart. You'd find another prize to chase after soon enough."

His expression blackened. "I have physical needs and desires just like every other man, and there have always been women ready to gratify them. Why should I deny it? But that fact of my past doesn't mean I don't envision something very different for my future."

He took another swallow of his brandy and went on. "Listen to me, Nicole, for I'm rapidly running out of patience. Don't mistake me for a fool. The contrast between mere physical attraction and love is quite distinct, and I'm just as capable of telling the difference as you. I know my own heart, and it's telling me that at last I've found someone to treasure—someone to protect and provide for the rest of my life. It's you who are denying your heart."

"No!" He was right, but some unshakable stubbornness in her would not let her admit it.

"Damm it," he cursed. In an instant he was next to her, twisting her head with his hands, forcing her to look at him. "I once said that it's better to face your fears and work through them," he said thickly, "and if that's what it takes with you . . ."

He kissed her with a fierce urgency that utterly dissolved her will to resist. Her own pent-up passion came roaring to life, and she returned his kiss with equal urgency.

They held each other for an age, as waves of feeling flooded over her. At last she pulled back from him, her large dark eyes glistening with moisture. "Yes," she whispered. "I love you."

His lips touched hers again, softly this time and tasting faintly of brandy. Slowly the pressure of his mouth grew more insistent and hers responded in kind. His gentle, stroking hands roamed her body, teasing her skin until it tingled.

With one strong arm around her back, his other swept below her legs. A moment later she was suspended in air as he crossed the room.

"Wait . . . where are . . ." she protested weakly.

"Wait? No, the world is ending tomorrow. Neither of us can wait any longer." His deep voice reverberated in his chest.

Yes, the time for waiting had passed. She slipped her arms around his neck and closed her eyes. A moment later the rhythm of his steps changed: they were going up a flight of stairs.

Then he was laying her on a soft mattress. She opened her eyes and saw the dark, rich material of a canopy over her. She had only an instant to take in the remainder of a masculine bedroom before she felt the mattress sinking beneath his weight as he sat down next to her.

One large hand cupped the side of her face. With his fingertips he brushed back the hair from her forehead, then traced the line of her jaw. He traced her lips, and his fingers were replaced by his mouth. Again Nicole was spinning in the swirling darkness of sensual delight.

He was lying next to her, his mouth never ceasing its exploration, his hand running enticingly up and down her body. It stopped only briefly, to flick apart the buttons of her blouse and sweep it open. Braless, her breasts were easy victims for the fiendishly sensuous, circular stroking of his hand. Her skin quivered beneath his touch.

A soft groan came from him. "My God, Nicole . . . please, you must stop me."

"I can't," she breathed, nor did she want him to. Never did she want to go back to the world of fumbling good-night kisses, of a promise that was never fulfilled. All

142

restraint had long since deserted her, and she pulled him close.

It was James who broke her embrace much later, sitting up with another soft groan. She gave a weak cry of protest, but the strength seemed to have left her limbs completely. She made no move as he pulled her sneakers from her feet; she heard them fall softly on the carpet somewhere across the room. Her blouse vanished magically from her shoulders.

Next he was tugging at her belt, and with one sweeping movement she was fully exposed to him. She heard his sharp intake of breath and saw the dark fire in his eyes as his seering gaze traveled up and down the length of her.

Involuntarily she reached for him, and he was lying next to her again, his clothes pleasantly rough against the tenderness of her exposed skin. Her hands slid up beneath his sweater, luxuriously running over the muscled surface of his back.

With maddening precision his hands and lips began to arouse her to a pitch of unbearable excitement. He was at once painfully gentle and deliciously demanding. She entered a liquid realm of pleasure, where only individual sensations stamped themselves on her memory: skin against skin, his hair tickling her belly, the unaccustomed weight of him.

Patiently he led her toward that time when wanting is no more. She followed willingly, marveling at the pleasure of yielding softly, of puzzles solved, of hidden places touched in love for the first time. It seemed impossible that she should wait any longer.

And then, distantly, a door slammed.

The sound was like the cold steel of a knife suddenly pressed against her skin. She froze, instantly immobile. James heard it too: he raised his head sharply and listened.

For a full minute there was deafening silence. Then, just as she had decided it had been her imagination, a faint female voice could be heard calling, "James? Are you there?"

Nicole's throat seemed to close suddenly, and she fought for breath. James muttered a curse under his breath. Rolling off the bed, he commanded, "Stay here. Don't move."

Pulling on the sweater he had discarded, James crossed the room in five long strides and went out the door, closing it quietly behind him.

The second she was alone Nicole was aware that she had to know . . . no matter what the cost. She sprang up off the warm surface of the bed and began gathering her clothes, suppressing her feelings of foolishness. Better to be a wise fool than an ignorant one.

After a frantic hunt she found her missing sneaker and pulled it on. Fully dressed, she moved to the door and opened it silently.

The hall was empty, but from the entrance below came the sound of voices. Quietly she moved to the top of the stairs and looked down.

James was standing with his back to her, a manila envelope in one hand and a sheaf of papers in the other. Standing next to him, her hand resting intimately on his forearm, was a woman in a tight red dress daringly slit to midthigh.

The woman's face was instantly familiar, but it took Nicole a moment longer to remember the name that went with it. When it came to her, it brought with it a rush of humiliating memories.

She was his secretary, Jackie Faulkner.

CHAPTER 7

Nicole stood frozen, taking in the scene with disbelief. Their conversation carried up the stairs clearly.

"This *could* have waited," James was saying, though there was nothing in his voice to suggest that he was annoyed by the interruption.

Jackie gave a little laugh. "You know I'll grab any excuse to come rushing out here. Now, aren't you going to give me a drink, darling?"

Darling! Nicole's stomach turned over. The whole situation was becoming sickeningly clear. Jackie wheeled and marched into the living room, showing a generous length of finely sculpted leg as she did. James followed close behind her like a trained terrier.

As they disappeared from sight, Nicole collapsed on the top step. The two of them had obviously played out this scenario before: the dedicated secretary bringing important business papers to her boss's home. The dedicated secretary being rewarded with a drink, an arm around the shoulder, a kiss. . . .

With a tiny groan she buried her face in her hands. The scene was too painful to complete. She had been an idiot to believe he would change the habits of a lifetime just for her.

But suppose Jackie's appearance was entirely innocent after all? Desperately she seized this thought, but rejected it again almost immediately. What secretary—no matter how devoted—played messenger at this time of night? And dressed in an evening gown, besides. No, Jackie had obviously come to deliver more than business papers.

Suddenly Nicole was overwhelmed by the need to get away, to run far from this house and the man who had brought her nothing but pain.

Gathering her wits, she crept down the stairs and tiptoed to the hall closet. Easing open the door, she took her poncho and tucked it under her arm. If she could only get out without being heard. . . .

"I thought I told you to stay put," James said behind her.

Startled, she spun around. His hands were tucked casually in his pockets, but his eyes flashed a sharp warning.

She could think of nothing to say. The sight of him sent hot and cold waves of longing and resentment through her in rapid succession. How could he bear to confront her like this, with his treachery so plainly exposed?

"Get back upstairs," he hissed.

"No! I'm not an idiot," she said loudly, as much for her own benefit as his. Part of her wanted to obey him, to dumbly wipe away all that she had seen and heard. But she fought against such a breach of dignity.

"Quiet," he whispered harshly, "or you'll prove otherwise. I'm only trying to save you from embarrassment." He gripped her arm with fingers of steel.

146

"You mean save yourself! If you cared a damn about me, you wouldn't have brought me here in the first place."

"That's the way, honey. You tell him!" Jackie said, appearing in the living room doorway.

James turned to her, his voice dark with anger. "Kindly stay out of this," he snapped.

"That's quite all right. Don't let me interrupt," Nicole blurted. She had intended to sound sarcastic, but the effect was spoiled by the sob rising in her throat. Shaking free of his grip, she raced to the door and out into the night.

Hurling herself past the Mercedes and the low-slung sports car parked next to it, she sped across the wide lawn. It had stopped raining, but the grass was still wet, and in a moment her sneakers were soaked through.

She ran on, oblivious. When she reached the end of the lawn, she cast a terrified glance backward, half expecting to see James coming after her. But he was not.

He was silhouetted in the warm yellow light of the front door, hands on hips, watching her go. Of course he would have no need to chase her. He already had a substitute conveniently at hand.

She turned and plunged heedlessly into a dense patch of woods. Wet branches slapped her face and her feet tangled in the undergrowth, but she hardly noticed. A minute later she broke through onto a paved surface: the entrance drive. It seemed to go on forever, but at last she was passing through the gate and onto the road.

On and on she ran, propelled by the horrible knowledge that she had come within minutes of becoming another of his conquests.

When Nicole awoke the next morning, every muscle in her body ached. Her head was throbbing, but she didn't mind the pain: it kept her mind off the events of the night before.

Just when she had thought she could run no farther, a pair of headlights had loomed up in front of her. At first she had feared it was James, but to her relief it was a police car. Mercifully the officer had driven her all the way to Mannihasset without asking more than a few perfunctory questions.

In retrospect it seemed odd that he had not been more inquisitive, but she supposed he was used to finding people in distress. No doubt she was not the first woman to be found running from the Benton estate in terror.

That morning it was a relief to be out on the water, safely supervising the intermediates under the broiling sun. Back in the club at lunchtime, though, she was constantly checking behind her, expecting James to materialize at any moment.

By five o'clock she was nearly convinced that he wouldn't appear. Snatching up her bag, she pulled the door of her office closed and hurried down the stairs, anxious to be on her way home. She zipped through the main entrance hall, carefully averting her eyes from the trophy case where the Benton Cup stood accusingly.

She was halfway across the footbridge when she saw James coming toward her. He was dressed in sailing clothes: khaki shorts, a white sport shirt, and Docksiders. It was useless to turn back, she saw: if she did, he would only corner her somewhere in the club.

Setting her jaw, she continued forward briskly, hoping he would let her pass without a challenge. But when she was only a few feet from him, he blocked her path.

She shot him a cold look, but it had no effect. In an even voice he said, "I'm glad to see that you got home without injury."

"No thanks to you," she shot back.

"Yes, Sergeant Harrison deserves the thanks," he agreed.

"Then you know. . . ." So, he even had the town police in his pocket! "How nice to have cops to do your chauffeuring chores for you. Well, if you're expecting thanks from me for simply dialing the phone, you can forget it. It was because of you that I was stranded out there in the first place!"

"Must I remind you that you came with me by choice?" he stated flatly.

"That's stretching it."

"Perhaps. But later in the evening you seemed anxious enough to stay, or must I remind you about that too?"

Nicole's eyes narrowed in fury. The man had no shame whatsoever! "No, I'd rather *not* be reminded of that. It certainly won't happen again."

"No? I would be sorry if that were true, though when you turn recalcitrant like this, I have a hard time remembering that I care."

"Then don't! That would make me very happy," she said bitterly, disbelieving her own words even as she spoke. The truth was that she wanted him more than ever. But he would never love her in the way she needed to be loved: singly, completely.

His expression was unreadable, but when he spoke, he seemed almost sad. "I think you know what would make you truly happy, though you won't admit it to yourself. Still, I've done all I can for the moment. Now it's up to you to face the facts."

The facts seemed very clear to her. Why did he think that further reflection would change her mind?

"Don't hold your breath," she said.

All at once his cool facade cracked. His eyes blazed

149

angrily, and he sucked in a long breath. "I'm a proud man, Nicole," he said. "Don't push me too far. Last night I thought we had finally resolved our differences. Now I find this isn't so. If there are any doubts, any questions left in your mind, ask them now. I'll do my best to answer."

The chilly warning implied in this command made her want to cower. But she stood her ground. There was no point in letting him explain himself: he would only weave his web of words around her again, as he had so often before.

Beneath their feet waves rushed in and out among the boulders supporting the bridge.

"Very well," he said at last, his voice icy with resolve. "There are three weeks left until the cup races. During that time I suggest we limit ourselves to a working relationship as before. Agreed?"

"Yes," she said firmly.

"Good. But after that, beware. I am going to use whatever means I feel are necessary to force you to accept what you already know to be true."

This open declaration of war shocked her. "And what is that?" she asked contentiously.

"That you're in love with me."

"No!" she spat. "I'll never admit that!"

"You don't have to," he said calmly. "You've already told me it's true in a hundred ways. What I said was that I will force you to *accept* the fact—a very different thing."

His cool assurance infuriated her, but she knew she could not allow herself the comfort of hoping that she could defeat him in a battle of wills. Hard experience had shown that he could do all he claimed.

"Okay. If you have nothing further to say, I'll be going," she declared. Without waiting for a reply, she pushed past him and marched off the footbridge.

A minute later she was furiously pedaling her bike home to the Petersens'.

The following weeks were just as James had promised. Not once did he let up the pressure at work, but neither did he allow a hint of their stormy private feud to show through. The possibility that he might finally have lost interest in her gave her no comfort, though. If anything, it increased her anguish.

Steve noticed the hunted look in her eye but mistook it for nerves over the upcoming Benton Cup. Emily Petersen seemed concerned about her too.

"Nicky, I don't see how it's possible, but I swear you've grown thinner lately. Why don't you have some dessert, dear?" she suggested gently at dinner one night.

"Dessert?" she echoed lamely. The meal had been delicious—broiled bluefish delicately seasoned with ginger and scallions—but she had forced down her portion only to avoid insulting Emily.

"Yes, we have vanilla ice cream and some lovely-looking raspberries to go over the top."

Raspberries! Nicole felt sick. Unlike her, however, Frank's appetite seemed to improve when he was under pressure.

"Ah, just what I needed!" he exclaimed with satisfaction after demolishing his portion. "Ugh, it's been beastly at work, I can tell you. The boss has been in a foul mood for weeks. I wonder what's got into him. You wouldn't happen to have any clues, would you, Nicky?" he asked slyly.

Nicole blanched. "No, I wouldn't know," she lied, hoping he wouldn't notice the tremor in her voice.

After all the concerned attention she was getting from

151

her friends, it was almost a relief to encounter James's cold demeanor the following day.

As usual he had taken charge of matters and was giving a short lecture to the Sacred Six prior to their final practice session. When he adopted his imperious manner, it was easy for her to remember why she disliked him so.

Yet neither could she forget that there had been times of tenderness and pleasure, laughter and easy companionship. Magically he also seemed to grow more handsome as time passed.

She studied his face in the clear morning light. Its classically cut features would lose none of their character with age. The lines would be deeper, of course, but it would still have its angular ruggedness. What would it be like to grow old with him?

She imagined them in autumn, walking arm in arm down a country road, scuffing through drifts of russet-colored leaves. There would be gray in his hair, and she would be wearing a scarf to keep herself warm in the crisp, cold air. There would be no need to speak: after so many years they would know each other's thoughts.

It was a pleasant fantasy, but no more than that, she knew. Her future would probably be very different. There was New York, first of all. There was no telling how many ways city life would change her.

New York. In less than two weeks she would be there. She quickly pushed this thought away, however. Somehow she couldn't bring herself to plan beyond the Benton Cup races the following week. Lurking in the background was the suspicion that she did not want to leave Mannihasset, to leave—

There was a figure standing over her—James. Reluctantly she forced herself back to reality.

"Where were you just then, I wonder?" A wry smile twisted his lips.

"*That* will have to remain a mystery," she said irritably. The last thing she wanted to admit was that she was daydreaming about him.

It was then she noticed that the room was empty. The Sacred Six had evidently been sent out to their dinghies.

She started to rise from her armchair, saying, "I'll warm up the Whaler."

"Stay a minute," James said.

Nicole sank back down as he dropped into a chair opposite her. "Well, what do you think our chances are?" he asked.

"You mean as far as the Benton Cup goes?" she said warily.

"Of course."

She pursed her lips. She had been so preoccupied lately that she hadn't stopped to give the matter much thought. On reflection, she realized that the situation looked far better than she had guessed it would at the start of the summer.

"I suppose it depends on the caliber of the competition," she said. "We have the advantage of familiarity with the local waters, of course. And our team has come a long way."

"True," he agreed. "But have they come far enough?"

"I'd rate them competitive, at least relative to my experience at that age. I think they might have given my college team a run for their money, in fact."

James considered her assessment. "Yes, they've done well," he remarked.

"Why do you ask? Surely you're not afraid we'll lose?"

"No," he confessed. "I was really more interested in

hearing your opinion. You seem rather . . . nervous lately."

No small wonder! With a cunning wolf prowling at her door, of course she was jumpy.

"Nicole," he said suddenly, "I know we agreed to leave private matters alone, but I think it might be wise to reopen the discussion at this point."

"Why?" Her feelings had not changed, she insisted to herself.

"Because your mind isn't on your work, among other reasons. You're distracted at a time when we need your full concentration."

"Well, that's not entirely my fault," she said defensively, crossing her arms in front of her.

"That's true," he admitted unexpectedly. "Our future could have been settled long before now if I hadn't been so impatient. It's amazing how consistently I lose my head over you, in fact. I ought to have seen from the beginning that my objectionable, heavy-handed attempts to seduce you were absolutely wrong."

"How do you know the 'right' methods wouldn't have produced the same result?" she said.

He ignored this gibe. "Nicole, for once be honest. End this contest with your heart. You're in love with me—you can't deny it."

Suddenly she was tired of resisting. It was simply too exhausting to continue arguing with him. "And what if I am?" she cried. "What difference would it make? How can I allow myself to love you if you don't love me in return?"

James leaned toward her, his voice painfully vulnerable. "Do you still believe that I don't?"

"You've never told me that you *do*!"

"Darling, I've tried to show you in every way I know how, regrettable though some of my actions may have been. Please try to understand," he pleaded. "Expressions of deep feeling don't come easily to me, but if the words make any difference, I'll say them: I love you. In more ways than I had thought possible."

"I—" Nicole choked, unable to reply. The cost and sincerity of this confession were undeniable. But could she hope to believe him? She desperately wanted to, yet she held back.

"You don't trust my words," he said, reading her mind. "I understand that. What we need is time. We could have a rare happiness together, Nicole. Let me show it to you."

She kept her eyes lowered, not trusting herself to look at him. He went on, "When the Cup races are over, when we can be together without interruption, let me show you how it can be. Will you?"

"Yes," she said in a small voice.

Only then did she allow herself to look up at him, her eyes half hopeful, half afraid. "Yes," she repeated.

"Thank God," he murmured. He came to her and took her hand in his and kissed it tenderly. "My love, the first moment our responsibilities here are finished—"

Approaching giggles in the hall interrupted them. James rose to his feet as Stu and Patty burst in.

"Hey, come on!" Patty said. "We're all ready to go."

"Right," James said, "so are we." Extending a hand, he helped Nicole up, and a minute later they were back at work.

It was a hard day, but Nicole was grateful for the distraction. She didn't want to think about the rash, impulsive commitment she had made.

Fortunately there was no time for reflection in the days that followed, either. With the three-day Benton Cup series less than a week away, Watch Point was swept up in a whirlwind of preparation. Announcements and applications had been mailed earlier in the summer, and now seventy-five crews from around the country would be arriving within a forty-eight-hour period.

Nicole was surprised to find that she wasn't expected to do much in the way of organization. Instead, a regular group of dedicated club members went into action. With an ease born of years of experience in coordinating the event, they found accommodations, organized registration teams, recruited the race committee, and tended to the ever-multiplying details.

For the club staff it was a hectic time as well. Steve had prepared for the influx of seventy-five additional dinghies by anchoring floating docks in the harbor. A small fleet of motorboats were borrowed to ferry the visiting crews back and forth to their boats.

Peter went into a delighted frenzy of activity, converting the dining room to a cafeteria-style buffet in order to handle the rotating shifts of racers at lunchtime. Nicole ran across him supervising the rearrangement of tables one morning.

"Ah-ha! There you are, *mon petit sauveur*!" he exclaimed, kissing her enthusiastically on either cheek.

"Peter!" she laughed. "What's that for?"

"Ho, as if you didn't know! That is for making me—us —happy again. The boss, you know, has been a growly bear for many weeks. It was intolerable: nothing could satisfy him. But now all has been put right again. No, no! Don't pretend you are ignorant of this. Excuse me. . . . No, Charlie, that table goes *there*!"

Nicole went on her way, shaking her head. She did not envy him his job. In addition to the visiting crews, there would be crowds of parents, spectators, and the yachting press to feed as well—many of whom, according to Steve, came specifically for the renowned Watch Point cuisine.

With her regular classes over and nothing more for her to do officially, Nicole began to volunteer for every unassigned job she could find. On the first morning of registration, the day before the actual cup eliminations were to begin, the vast main lounge had been cleared of furniture. Measurements had been marked on the floor with tape, and Nicole spent the morning on her hands and knees, laying sails against the markings to see that they conformed to regulations. Lines of chattering young sailors crowded the other end of the room, receiving their float assignments and race circulars.

A crowded skippers' meeting followed lunch, and late that afternoon a practice race was run to enable the visiting crews to tune their boats. Nicole ran the "lead" boat— the Whaler with a tall international orange pennant lashed to its stern. Driving in compass-straight lines, she went around the course in advance of the racers to show the direct route from mark to mark.

By the end of the first two days of racing, the fleet of eighty boats had been divided into two divisions, with one half eliminated from the actual cup competition. Two races of the final series of five had been run, and as the tired youngsters stowed their gear and wandered away with their parents for a night of much-needed rest, Nicole studied the large sheets of race results posted on the official bulletin board in the main lounge.

With her pocket calculator she tabulated the results. Although the sky had been clear and sunny for two days, the winds had fluctuated, which resulted in wild swings in the standings as each crew's luck changed. Alan Wentworth and Paul Bendix had made it to the finals, she saw.

But what gave her most satisfaction was the discovery that the team of Cindy and Todd Bowman was also high in the standings. They might only have had luck with the wind, of course, but nevertheless they had a chance of winning. *Someone* from Watch Point had to win!

"Well, what do you think?" boomed a deep, familiar voice next to her.

James! Oddly he had not appeared at the club since the week before, which had made it much easier for her to keep her tumultuous emotions in check. Now she found her heart racing wildly.

She forced her voice to remain calm, however. Turning to him, she said in her most professional manner, "It's too early to say anything definite, I think. No one has been placing high with any consistency. It's anybody's trophy yet."

"Hmmm . . ." He studied her, one hand rubbing his chin thoughtfully. His dark eyes were alight with mischief, but he asked seriously, "And how are you holding up?"

"Me? Just fine, thanks. Why shouldn't I be?" she said brightly, feeling far less conviction than her words implied. If only he wouldn't look at her in quite that way!

"You haven't forgotten your promise? Tomorrow night the racing will be over. Then . . ." He left the thought tantalizingly incomplete.

"No, I haven't forgotten," she said, swallowing.

Though she was dead tired, it wasn't until the early hours that she fell asleep that night. She had deliberately done all she could to keep her mind off James and the possibilities he presented. Fear of disappointment and a wild excitement battled for her attention, but she resolutely forced these feelings out of her mind.

The next day dawned gray and overcast. A storm was threatening, but it held off for the first two races that morning. The winds were high, though, and the race committee prudently hoisted a life jacket, thus requiring the racers to wear theirs.

Nicole dutifully drove the lead boat in each race, too anxious to relinquish the job to a replacement. Dressed in her bulky yellow foul-weather gear, she sat in the pitching Whaler, tabulating the results of the fourth race. Marking the scores on her clipboard, she saw that the results were still too close to call. A dozen crews—including Cindy and Todd, as well as Alan and Paul—all had a chance. The final race would decide the outcome.

As the forty dinghies tacked out of the harbor after lunch, the wind howled. Bucking up and down over the waves, the little boats heeled far over, their crews hiking out over the water to keep them in control. Wisely the race committee shortened the final race to a simple triangular course, for skillful boat handling would count more than clever tactics in these conditions.

As the starting sequence began, Nicole started her run to the first mark. The fleet of spectator boats had diminished considerably, and the race committee had exchanged their snappy white pants and blue blazers for rain gear. Nevertheless Nicole felt a surge of excitement, a keen sense of the occasion, as the starting cannon boomed and a long line of dinghies moved across the starting line at once.

Conditions were still manageable at the start, but by the time the first boats rounded the leeward mark for the final downwind run, the wind had begun to overpower many of the crews. Some abandoned the race altogether, heading straight for the harbor. Others luffed their sails heavily, hoping only to finish the race.

The final leg of the race was a disaster. As spinnakers were raised, popping out of their bags and snapping full of wind instantly, many of the boats began to broach. The young crews struggled, and several boats capsized.

Nicole raced to help, shouting reassurances to the swimming youngsters as she picked them up. The shrieking of the wind and high waves added to the confusion, but fortunately, with the aid of several of the spectator boats, the floundering crews were all rescued safely.

Miraculously a number of the dinghies completed the race, but with a boatload of wet, shivering sailors to ferry back to the harbor Nicole did not see the finish. It wasn't until later that afternoon, after she had changed into dry clothes herself, that she was able to go to the bulletin board and check the results.

She couldn't believe her eyes at first. Then she thanked heaven for the heavy-weather training on which James had insisted. Not only had Cindy and Todd finished the race under the worst possible conditions, they had won! And with it they had won the Benton Cup for Watch Point once again.

The awards banquet that night was jubilant, in spite of the near-disasters. Cindy and Todd beamed, their new-found confidence making them seem older than they were. Alan and Paul had tied for sixth overall, each earning himself a plaque, which fortunately was enough to satisfy Alan's abrasive father. Thanks and congratulations were heaped on Nicole, but she barely heard them.

Her only thoughts were for James. Now that the hour of reckoning had come, she knew she was glad she had promised herself to him.

As the evening wore on, though, her elation faded. Even though he had no official reason to attend, she had assumed he would be present at the awards banquet. But he did not appear. She waited through the awards, waited as the crowd thinned and the dining room was cleared. She waited until after midnight, until she was practically the only person left.

Still he did not appear. Slowly she was hit by the crushing fact that he was not coming for her. After all, why should he? She had served her purpose, her job was done. There was no real reason to string her along anymore.

She had been a fool to believe he genuinely cared. He had said he loved her, but what proof was that coming from a man like him?

At last Peter was switching off the lights, preparing to lock up. With her heart in shreds, her mind numb, Nicole went out into the night.

CHAPTER 8

Starting at the top of her dresser, Nicole pulled open each of its drawers in rapid succession, hastily double-checking to be sure that they were indeed empty. They were.

Now it only remained for her to fold and pack the clothes hanging in her closet. She glanced inside her steamer trunk, which sat on the floor near the end of the bed, its top flung back. Fortunately there was still plenty of room.

After a restless night relieved only by brief snatches of shallow, unrefreshing sleep, Nicole had gratefully climbed out of bed as soon as daylight appeared in her window. During the night she had become increasingly certain that the only sane course of action left open to her was to leave Mannihasset as soon as possible.

There was no reason for her to stay. Sailing classes were over and the Benton Cup had been successfully defended once again. She was required to write an end-of-season report and evaluation, but that could be done in New York and mailed back to the club.

Steve would be left with the tiresome job of dismantling and storing the dinghies for the winter, of course, but that couldn't be helped. The sooner she was away, the sooner she could begin the impossible task of forgetting James.

At breakfast the Petersens had been upset when she announced her plan.

"So soon! But, Nicky," Emily had protested unhappily, "aren't you going to give yourself a proper vacation?"

"Perhaps she's fed up with us," Frank grumbled.

Horrified, she assured them she would miss them both very much, but that she simply had to go. They had tried to change her mind for several minutes more, but Nicole wouldn't be swayed.

At last Frank had concluded the discussion by asking, "At least promise me you won't vanish before I come home from work tonight, okay?"

She assured him she would not. Indeed, she had to rely on him to drive her to the train at Boston's South Street Station, as Emily did not drive.

Still disgruntled, Frank had then stalked out to his car, muttering, "We'll get to the bottom of this soon enough," though Nicole did not hear him.

Now she was nearly packed and had only to decide which items to bring with her in a smaller suitcase. She would have to leave her trunk and bicycle with the Petersens until she had found an apartment in New York, but she didn't think they would mind.

New York. Contrary to her earlier feelings of dread, she had almost convinced herself that she was looking forward to the dirt and distraction of the city. She smiled grimly at the irony of it.

Looking aimlessly around the room, she noticed that she had neglected to clean off the tiny desk that stood below the rear window. Gloomily she began shuffling through the odds and ends that had collected there over the summer.

Outside it was a perfect August day. Under any other circumstances she would not have been able to resist the temptation to go sailing or exploring on her bike, but now she relentlessly forced her attention back to the business of packing.

Just then the sound of upraised voices came from downstairs. She couldn't hear them clearly, but judging from their tone, there was an argument going on. Should she check on the situation? What if Emily was in trouble?

Before she could reach a decision, however, she heard the sound of footsteps racing up the stairs . . . coming too fast to belong to either of the Petersens, she realized. Instinctively she froze, her heart thumping.

The intruder took the stairs leading to her room three at a time. The door shot open and there stood James, dressed in a pair of tan slacks and a blue sport shirt that stretched revealingly over his muscled chest.

Instantly the room was charged with electricity. Why had he come? Part of Nicole fervently wished he had not. She did not feel strong enough to survive the stormy emotions he stirred in her; it would almost be easier to live with the misery of never seeing him again.

But as she stared at his familiar figure the ache in her heart told her that she was glad, after all. Somehow the pain would be worthwhile just for the brief joy of being near him for a moment.

James glanced around the room, quickly assessing the scene with fiery eyes. A bolt of anger flashed across his face but vanished just as quickly. When he turned to her, it was with a chilling air of resolution.

Nicole knew she couldn't stand up against the ruthless logic of one of his verbal attacks. But he did not speak.

Instead he crossed the room with a few long strides, gathered her in his arms, and kissed her.

It was like waking from a dream. For a shocking instant it seemed as if nothing in the whole of her experience had been real except the feeling of his lips pressing down forcefully on hers. All the anguish of the past few hours vanished as if it had never been.

They held each other for what seemed like hours. For Nicole it was a time of revelation. As she floated in the safe circle of his arms, she realized how childish it had been to fight against him. Surrender was so sweet, and so right.

When at last she returned to the world of time and solid objects, she felt profoundly changed. Her head rested in the hollow of his shoulder, and she could feel his fingers combing through her short, wispy hair. She looked up at him with questioning eyes.

"Why is it that I'm always driving like a maniac to find you?" he asked with a weak, relieved laugh. "When I stopped in the plant this morning and Frank told me that you were leaving for New York, I thought I was going to lose my mind."

She hugged him tightly. "I'm sorry," she said into his chest. "I don't want to hurt you."

"Then you shouldn't have tried to run away," he scolded gently, raising her chin with his fingertips. "Did you think I wouldn't keep my word?"

Her heart contracted guiltily. Indeed, she had not shown the smallest amount of trust in him. "When you disappeared last night, I didn't know what to think," she explained weakly.

"My absence was unavoidable. If only you weren't so impetuous, you would have learned why today. But we can wipe away everything that's happened before this moment if you want to. Do you? Tell me . . . will you go with me wherever I ask?"

"Yes!" she breathed, and then she was lost again in the swirling sensation of his kiss.

Some time later James disengaged himself from her, leaving her with the odd feeling of being cast adrift, even though her feet were still planted firmly on the floor.

"As enjoyable as this is," he said, "I'm afraid we'll have to restrain ourselves. We have to get on the road right away."

"On the road! But where . . . ?"

"Hush, my love. There really isn't time for lengthy explanations. Will you simply do as I say and accept the fact that I must handle things in this way?"

"Of course," she answered.

"Good." Looking around at the disarray, he said in a lighter tone, "Unfortunately, though, I can't let you indulge your feminine instinct to pack for every contingency. Do you have a duffel bag?"

"Yes, but—"

"Get it out," he interrupted.

She did as he told her without further protest. Following his directions, she packed enough light, functional clothing for a week. Zipping her green nylon duffel bag closed a few minutes later, she stood up and announced, "I'm ready, I guess."

James was standing impatiently in the middle of the room, his head clearing the low ceiling by only a few inches. Oddly the cozy attic that she had come to love in the past few months now seemed absurdly small and unfamiliar—almost as if she had never lived there at all.

"If you've forgotten anything, don't worry. There'll be some time to shop later," he assured her. "Let's go."

Obediently she picked up her bag and followed him

downstairs. She had no idea where he was taking her, nor did she want to know. Love had suddenly become an adventure and she wanted to savor the delicious thrill of venturing into the unknown.

An anxious-looking Emily was waiting in the hall.

"I'm sorry I was short with you a minute ago, Emily," James apologized. "I thought I was losing a vital crew member because of a misunderstanding."

"Crew!" Nicole and Emily exclaimed together.

He gave Nicole a let-me-handle-this look. To Emily he said, "Yes, I'm running *Warlord* in the Newport–Nassau race, which begins tomorrow, and I was lucky enough to recruit Nicole for some of the foredeck work."

Instantly the perplexity vanished from Emily's face, taking some of the wrinkles with it. "Ah! So that's the reason for the sudden departure. But, Nicky," she complained, "why didn't you just explain?"

"I'm afraid she was being considerate to a fault," James answered for her. "No doubt she thought you would be shocked to hear that she would be spending several days at sea with an unmarried man."

"Nonsense," Emily declared, giving Nicole a reproving glance. "We're quite up-to-date in our views, I think."

"With seven other crew members to play chaperone, there was no cause for worry in any case," James added. "Now, Frank tells me that you'll be able to keep her things for a bit?"

"Yes, yes. For as long as need be," she assured him. "I'm certain Nicky won't be in a hurry to leave the Bahamas!"

"Excellent! Emily, you are the soul of understanding," he said smoothly.

Nicole could do no more than mechanically return Emily's knowing wave as they started down the street.

Her head was still spinning from the rapid turn of events. It wasn't until some time later, as they followed Interstate 95 south toward Rhode Island, that the situation began to come into focus.

Sailing in the exclusive Newport–Nassau race was mind-bending but disappointing at the same time. Sailing a thoroughbred yacht like *Warlord* would take every ounce of the crew's skill and concentration. Nicole's fantasies of leisurely moonlit nights alone with James vanished.

As if reading her thoughts, he gave her a long, sideways look. "It's going to be hard work," he said coolly.

"I know," she answered.

She owed him that. All summer long she had acted like a spoiled child: opposing him at every opportunity, rejecting his every advance. That he had persisted was a miracle, but it was certain that he wouldn't easily forget her foolishness.

No, she needed to prove herself to him now. To be strong and reliable instead of unpredictable and rash. To work with him instead of against him. To be the woman he could love for a lifetime instead of the girl who had intrigued him one summer. . . .

Carefully she began to ask technical questions about the boat. Pleased by her interest, James answered them in detail. His disappearance the night before, she discovered, had been due to the arrival of a new computerized navigation system, the installation of which had required his presence in Newport.

"Tell me about the rest of the crew," she asked after a while.

James smiled. "I've been sailing with most of them for a number of years. They're a very dedicated bunch. Some of them know the boat better than they know their own wives, I think."

"They're all men?"

"Yes. Does that worry you?"

Nicole considered before answering. Being the one woman on a boat full of men would be an odd experience to say the least! Yet if it proved to be embarrassing, she would simply have to overcome her feelings. She was the one who had always maintained that she could sail as well as any man, after all.

"No, if you're not concerned, then I won't be either," she said finally. A new thought struck her. "Won't they think I'm bad luck?"

"Taking a woman to sea, and all that? No, I don't think anyone believes that old superstition anymore. The fact is you're an excellent sailor, and that will become apparent quickly enough. Some of the wives concerned may blink, perhaps," he laughed, "but if any of them kick up a fuss, we'll invite them along too! That will shut them up; they know it will be anything but a party."

"And if any of the crew lays a hand on me, you'll keelhaul them anyway, right?"

He glanced at her, trying to decide if she was joking or not. "Probably, though I doubt the problem will come up," he said.

"I hope I'll be able to pull my weight."

"You will," he replied simply. Nicole settled back in her seat and closed her eyes, letting the cool breeze from the air conditioner wash over her.

"Watch your head!" someone called.

Nicole crouched down on the deck and ducked as Foggy Faraday and Bill Leighton carried aboard *Warlord*'s graphite boom. When it had passed overhead, Nicole turned her attention back to the deck-mounted sheeves

169

she was spraying with silicone oil and wiping clean with a rag.

For the past twenty-four hours *Warlord*'s crew had been working nonstop to get through the hundreds of necessary prerace maintenance chores, safety checks, and double checks. Now, with only an hour to go before they were due to cast off for the start of the race, activity had reached a feverish pitch.

When she and James had pulled up at the end of Bannister's Wharf the day before, they had been greeted immediately by a man with a long doggish face and blond hair curling around his ears.

"There you are!" he called.

"Sorry, but I'm a bit behind schedule," James apologized as they stepped from the car. "Nicole, this is Foggy Faraday, our navigator, weather-bird, and slave master. He'll assign you your prerace duties. Foggy, this is our new number nine, Nicole Tanner."

With not a trace of surprise Foggy gave her hand a perfunctory shake and said, "You're just in time. We've got a helluva lot to get through today."

They followed Foggy through the security gate at the end of the wharf and down the dock to where *Warlord* was tied, half a dozen rubber bumpers keeping it from chafing against the dock. The crew was easy to recognize in their red Lacoste shirts with the boat's name stitched in tiny letters on the front. Several of them were hunched over a deck winch that they had taken apart for lubrication, and someone else was halfway up the mast in a sling.

"Listen up, swabs!" Foggy shouted. "We've got a new addition to the crew. This is Nicole. These guys are Bill Leighton, Alex, Harris, and the guy up the mast is Smokin' Shapiro," he said, pointing to each one in turn.

There was a chorus of hellos, and those who could came up to shake hands.

"What a refreshing change, Benton," said one. "I see you have some taste in women after all."

Nicole colored, but no one seemed to notice. Though no two looked alike, they were all big men with the tanned faces and crow's-feet around the eyes that came from years of squinting into the sun and wind. Curiously they all seemed older than James.

Foggy chased them quickly back to work and started leafing through a list a dozen pages long on his clipboard. "All right, we'll start you off with something easy." He brought Nicole down the dock a few yards to a pile of coiled lines that came up to her waist.

"Sheets and assorted lines," Foggy said, writing her name down next to the item on his list. "They have to be inspected for frayed and worn spots. If you find any, put those lines into a separate pile. We'll need to cut and whip replacements by the end of the day."

Nicole stared at the pile, bug-eyed. It would take hours!

"It's a tedious job, but an essential one," James said sympathetically. "We can't afford any equipment failures when we're fifty miles from shore in the middle of a blow."

"Get to it," Foggy ordered. Taking James by the arm, he led him back up the dock, discussing sails. Pulling up a milk crate, Nicole sat down and went to work, stopping every few minutes to sneak another look at the boat.

Warlord was breathtaking. Up close it appeared smaller than in its pictures, but its sleek, menacing profile was still awesome. Its deck was flush to lessen wind resistance, meaning that there would be uncomfortably low head clearance in the cabin below. The pitch black hull was perfectly smooth and polished to a deadly sheen. Somehow, in spite of its state-of-the-art hardware, it had a primeval, animal look. Like a shark, Nicole decided.

She did not see James again until eight that evening when the crew gathered for dinner at the fashionable Black Pearl restaurant. Laughing and joking, they were obviously glad to be back together again. Amid hearty applause, she was presented with her own *Warlord* shirt by Foggy.

Although everyone in the crew except James was married, only Foggy's wife, a tall blond named Betsy, had come down for the start of the race.

"It's so *boring* beforehand," she explained when Nicole questioned her. "You're lucky if you have ten minutes with your man, so most of the wives don't bother. They fly down for the finish in Nassau," she added slyly. "That's *much* more fun!"

"Do you ever do any ocean racing yourself?" Nicole asked.

"Never! I see how worn out Foggy looks at the end of one of these events, and he's got the stamina of a bull too. That kind of punishment's not for me, thanks," she answered, looking at Nicole curiously.

The crew had an invitation to a prerace dance that night at one of the fabled Bellevue Avenue mansions, but by mutual consent they all returned to their hotel rooms. They would need to be up early in the morning, for there was still much to be done.

Nicole was left alone with James while he paid the bill with a credit card. As they stepped outside, she looked at him expectantly.

"Much as I disliked doing so, I've booked us into separate hotel rooms," he announced. "Even if it's going to be a milk run all the way to Nassau, we'll need to be well rested."

172

Nicole nodded somberly and gave him a quick crushing hug in reply.

When a call from the front desk woke her at a shockingly early hour the next morning, she understood the wisdom of his restraint. While the rest of Newport was still rubbing the sleep out of its eyes, she was already at Bannister's Wharf being weighed together with her duffel bag.

Now, with only a few minutes left until they were to cast off, Nicole was wiping the excess silicone oil from the last of the sheeves. A large crowd of wealthy-looking friends-of-friends, journalists, and gawkers had managed to slip past the security gate over the course of the morning, making the last-minute loading of backup equipment and coolers of food even more hectic.

In contrast to all this glamorous activity she was glad to see that the battered-looking oyster boats had not stopped unloading their cargo at the Aquidneck Lobster Company's shed next door. She preferred the honest noise of cranky winches and conveyer belts to the superficial conversation of the spectators.

The sight of her in her red crew shirt had caused a good deal of ill-concealed amusement and speculation, and she was anxious to leave for the comparative quiet of open water.

At last it seemed as if they might be ready to go. The crew all stood on deck as Foggy ticked off the final items on his list.

"Tanner!" he called suddenly. "We need a box of cooking stuff from the front seat of my car." He tossed Nicole the keys.

Glad to have a task that would take her out of sight for a few minutes, she pushed her way down the dock. Out in the parking lot she found Foggy's car and retrieved the box of utensils. Just as she was about to return through the security gate, however, she heard a sharp hiss of indrawn breath behind her.

"Still playing sailor, I see!" There was no mistaking the venomous tones of Sheilah Pritchard.

Turning, Nicole saw the unpleasant sneer on her face. As usual she was dressed stunningly: her pristine white slacks were molded perfectly to her legs, and her red silk shirt was left daringly unbuttoned. Thin gold chains flashed brightly against the dark tan of her skin.

"Hello, Miss Pritchard," Nicole said stonily, her blood freezing in her veins.

Tossing back her long silver-blond hair with the habitual flip of her head, Sheilah rapidly took in Nicole's red crew shirt and the box of utensils she was carrying. "No doubt Jimmy is thrilled to have a girl who knows her place is in the kitchen—but I wouldn't carry the act too far."

"And why not?" She could feel her fragile fantasy life collapsing like a house of cards.

"Listen, you're a nice sort of kid, so I'm going to be straight with you," Sheilah went on in her poisonous voice. "The fact is that Jimmy and I have been lovers for a long time, and in fact we're going to be announcing our engagement soon. Granted he may be having some fun with you—Jimmy will have his little obsessions—but when the fun is over, he always comes back for the real thing. So why don't you save yourself some trouble and stay away from him, hmmm?"

With that, she pushed through the gate and flounced down the dock in the direction of *Warlord*.

Quivering with rage and humiliation, Nicole followed at a distance, but was not too far behind to witness Sheilah dramatically flinging her arms around a surprised James.

Brushing past them, Nicole hopped aboard the boat and

rushed down through the cabin hatch, slamming down the box near the tiny alcohol stove.

Sheilah's words stabbed at her again and again . . . *lovers* . . . *engagement* . . . *little obsessions.*

Had her feelings blinded her completely? Somehow she had managed to block out Sheilah's existence altogether . . . but evidently James had not.

Nicole was caught in a storm of confusion. James had been so tender, so sincere. She was sure he loved her. Yet the facts were undeniable: according to Sheilah they were almost engaged. Whether that was true, one thing was certain: James was keeping his options open.

She should have escaped his clutches while she had the chance. Now it was too late. They were about to cast off. There was no way that she could quit the crew at the last minute without making a fool of herself.

Miserably she went up on deck and took her place, resolutely fixing her gaze ahead. If there was to be a revolting farewell scene between James and Sheilah, she did not care to see it.

At last she heard James call, "Cast off!" Obediently she bent down and unwrapped the mooring line from its cleat and tossed it onto the dock. In front of them a cabin cruiser fired its engine, a towline went taut, and *Warlord* pulled smoothly away from the dock to cheers and shouts of "Good luck!" from the crowd.

A minute later they were out in the middle of Newport Harbor, with the entire city spread around them: the crowded wharfs and marinas, the Navy base, the lawns of breathtaking houses sweeping down to the water. The scene changed perspective with cinematic precision as they were towed through the water.

Nicole felt oddly removed from it all. There was none of the pounding thrill she usually experienced when setting out to sea. She was aware only of the bitter knowledge that James had betrayed her.

All too soon they were past Fort Adams in open water, being pulled into the wind by their escort. James gave the order to raise the sails, and Nicole sprang to lend a hand, her impassive face showing none of the torment that was raging inside her.

By the time they had been at sea for two days, life aboard the boat had settled into a familiar routine.

Foggy had assigned Nicole to the relatively easy day-time watch, when her most taxing responsibility was setting new foresails as wind conditions altered. The deck tossed and shifted beneath her feet, forcing her to move with careful deliberation, always catching her balance and reaching for handholds. She hated to think what would happen if she fell overboard—they would probably leave her behind.

No sacrifice was too great for the sake of speed. Not a single opportunity to fine-tune the boat was lost. When not scrambling on deck, Nicole was in the crew cockpit with the rest of her watch, her eyes fixed on the sails, constantly trimming them to take advantage of the tiny fluctuations in the wind.

She loved every minute of it. The sails towered overhead gracefully, brilliant white in the sunlight. When they raised the gigantic, multicolored spinnaker, it seemed to fill half the sky. *Warlord* churned through the water at incredible speed, leaving a roaring white wake behind it. At night she was lulled by the sound of water rushing past the hull.

And always there was the sea—now tranquil, now seething; now gray and steely, now a luminous blue-green; always changing, always the same.

More than anything it had been the sight of the unending sea that had brought Nicole to her senses. Riding the swells, with all the petty concerns of the world far away, it had been impossible to stay angry.

In the crowded, confined space of the boat she and James had not been able to exchange anything more than the most necessary words, but nevertheless it seemed as if they had been carrying on a silent dialogue all the same. He had known the effect the sea would have on her. It was his ultimate weapon, and she now sensed why she had not simply deserted on the dock at Newport.

Isolated on the vast expanse of the ocean, locked together with James inside the unbroken ring of the horizon, she had no choice but to come to terms with her feelings for him. She loved him deeply, completely. No longer was it possible to deny the fact, or hope to run away, or drive her feelings out with anger.

As the sun circled from horizon to horizon she reviewed the events of the summer. What a fool she had been to pass up the opportunities he had given her! Time and time again she had childishly refused him, afraid to be led into the unknown territories of passion.

It was no wonder that he turned to the likes of Sheilah Pritchard to satisfy his needs. She had wanted an equal exchange: for James to show the same, single-minded obsession she had for him. He had, in his own way, but she had been too naive to see it.

Could she hope that he still cared for her? In spite of her rebuffs he had pursued her all summer but perhaps only because they were constantly thrown together. Masculine pride would compel him to continue trying to seduce her long after any genuine feeling for her had died.

Nicole longed to confess everything to him, to beg for some sign of understanding or compassion. But it was impossible for them to be alone, so she could only trust in the power of her love.

Love. After all, what else mattered? When at last she had fully accepted the condition of her heart—as he had said she would—a welcome peacefulness settled over her. Where loving James had once meant unending torment, it now seemed a form of gentle ecstasy.

Perhaps he still loved her in return, perhaps not. It didn't matter. Somehow having loved him so profoundly was enough. If he broke her heart, she would still know that just once in her life she had experienced the rarest, most exalted emotion of all.

"Bring in that jib a bit. Ease up on the boom vang . . . not much . . . that's it." James stood squarely in his position behind the wheel. He gave his orders crisply, as if he weren't at all tired.

How did he do it? Nicole was exhausted, and although no one complained, she could tell from their drawn, unshaved faces that the rest of the crew were also feeling the effects of the days of hard sailing. Dawn had found them in a calm sea, but the wind had increased steadily all day, and her arms ached from changing sail after sail.

As if it sensed that the journey was almost over, *Warlord* was flying across the water, which had turned an astonishing turquoise color.

"Shouldn't be long now," Nicole heard Foggy say behind her.

The light color of the water indicated that they would be sighting land soon. The rest of the crew glanced toward the horizon anxiously, but Nicole kept her eyes fixed on the sails. As tired as she was, she somehow dreaded the end of the race.

Nassau would be her proving ground. If James would

178

let her, she would try to undo a whole summer's worth of stubborn rejection. Chances were, though, he would finally cast her aside in disgust. She had certainly given him reason enough.

Her stomach tightened at this thought, and she resolutely forced her mind back to the task at hand. The crew had long since discovered that she was a serious sailor, but her unfailing energy had surprised even the most chauvinistic among them. If only they knew it was born of desperation!

"Take a rest, Nick. You're making the rest of us look like shirkers," someone had said.

Nicole had only smiled in reply. The only real concession to her femininity had been a curtain hung discreetly across her bunk so that she could change in private, and as if to emphasize her lack of privilege, most of the crew had taken to calling her Nick.

"Land ho!" someone shouted gaily. All eyes turned to the horizon and after a minute she saw it, a brown smudge on the lip of the sea. A weak cheer went up.

As they drew closer the land began filling in more of the horizon. When they could distinguish blue hills in the distance and sparkling white beaches, someone called, "Helicopter!"

A tiny speck in the sky rapidly grew into a small red and white helicopter. It made a tight circle overhead, as if checking their sail number, and went zipping back toward land.

"All right! We must be the first in!" exclaimed Smokin' Shapiro.

"We'll see," James commented. Foggy had said they were making good time, but there was no way to know whether they were winning, for they had not seen another sail since the first day.

But there was no doubt as they crossed the finish line just outside Nassau harbor. On the committee boat a cannon boomed, sending off a puff of white smoke, and the spectator boats crowding the area hooted their horns madly.

The crew whooped and cheered, waving thank you and snapping open cans of cold beer. Foggy ruffled Nicole's hair and congratulated her with a hug. A speedboat pulled up alongside.

"Congratulations, *Warlord*!" called a race official through a megaphone. "You're the first to finish, and it looks like you'll be first on corrected time as well. We've had radio contact with your closest competitor, *Scaramouche,* and they're still three or four hours out!"

A new round of shouting went up from the crew, and the jubilation continued all the way in to their berth in the harbor. A large crowd had gathered, and when all the sails had been lowered and the boat secured, champagne was passed around while the crew gaily hugged and kissed their wives.

It was a long time before the crowd of well-wishers around James thinned. When it looked as if he might at last be free, Nicole made her way over to him, her heart hammering in her chest.

He regarded her warily, but after a moment his expression softened. It was faint encouragement, but she took it. She put her arms around him and squeezed.

"Ouch! Hold on there, you're really getting some muscles!" he said, drawing away.

She could not bear to let him go, however. She clung to his arm, not knowing where to begin. There was so much she wanted to say to him.

"Darling, I—" she said, but got no farther, for at that

moment a shrill, distinctive voice sounded above the noisy celebration like a siren.

"Yooo . . . Jiiiimmmmy!"

Nicole felt her heart being sliced neatly in two. Threading her way down the dock came Sheilah, dressed in tight white shorts and a colorful halter top that drew stares from every man in sight.

Flipping back her silver-blond mane, she rudely brushed Nicole out of the way and wrapped her arms around James. "Darling! I'm so happy for you!"

Nicole didn't wait to hear the rest. A weary sense of defeat overwhelmed her. Without seeing the black look on James's face, she slipped below and took her duffel bag from her bunk. Walking carefully along the outside of the boat, she made her way to the head of the slip and hopped off onto the dock, on the far side of the crowd. Unnoticed, she walked quietly out of the marina and into the waterfront streets of Nassau.

The city was like no place she had ever been, but she hardly noticed her surroundings as she wandered aimlessly along, alternately numb and fighting back tears.

She passed smelly fishing boats unloading their cargo, shaded outdoor cafés, swank shops, and street vendors. Young men on mopeds whistled at her, and large brown matrons clicked their tongues and shook their heads as she passed.

She passed by grand high-rise hotels with uniformed doormen, and squalid slums where the unemployed sat on stoops. She was oblivious of it all.

Some hours later she found herself sitting on a stone bench at the edge of a pristine white beach, empty now as the sun inched below the horizon. Trim, low villas in pastel shades stood across a road behind her, washed in the rosy colors of the sunset.

She had stopped crying and her throat was dry. A short distance down the road a boy in cutoff canvas pants was selling ices from a cart, but she had no money.

Whenever she tried to think her situation through logically, she always came back to the same humiliating, incontrovertible facts. The race was over, but the victory she had won over herself seemed hollow now. She had lost something far more important: the affection and respect of the man she loved.

She knew now that running away had been a mistake. In her hurt and anger she had forgotten her resolve to be steadfast, to prove herself to him. She desperately wanted to go back, but how could she face him now?

As it happened, though, James found her at that moment.

He was dressed as he had been that afternoon, but his cool, triumphant expression had been replaced by a haunted, hollow-eyed look of worry. He was holding a bright green ice in a paper cone.

"You look like you could use this," he said kindly. "I hope you like lime, It was all he had left."

She accepted it gratefully as he sat down next to her. Strangely, being with him was not painful. With her emotions exhausted she was only mildly curious about why he had come to look for her. She sucked on the shaved ice, savoring the cool liquid that trickled down her throat.

The sun slipped below the horizon, sending off its final blaze of color. James said wearily, "You know, if I weren't so relieved to find you, I think I'd make good on my promise to break every single bone in your body."

That wouldn't make me feel any worse than I do now, she thought to herself. Aloud, she said only, "I see."

James exploded. Grabbing her by the shoulders, he shook her fiercely. "Is that all you can say? It's taken me two frantic hours to find you. I've been sick with worry! When I realized that you had wandered off, I thought I would quite literally go mad."

"Oh, why don't you just leave me *alone*!" she cried. She wanted nothing more than for him to stay, but she was still too wounded to realize this.

James drew his hand through his thick dark hair in exasperation. "My God, Nicole. You blow hot and cold, and for the life of me I don't know why. If only you would explain."

"Would you understand? I don't think so. You're too used to having women fall at your feet to see why I don't."

A glimmer of understanding crept into his face. "You still think I'm an incorrigible playboy, don't you?"

"Are you going to deny it?"

"Yes. Oh, I don't pretend that there haven't been women in my life. On the contrary, there have been too many."

"But now it's different?" she mocked angrily. "All the others faded into insignificance when you met me, right?"

"Yes, that's right, believe it or not," he insisted. "I love you. *Only* you."

"And Sheilah Pritchard?"

Faced with the truth, he did not react as she expected. He did not stammer or smoothly try to explain away her charge.

Instead he laughed, a full, incredulous laugh. "Nicole, don't tell me you've been torturing yourself over *that* creature! Surely you have a higher opinion of me than that."

The color of the fading sunset disguised the flush on her face. "But she goes everywhere with you. How am I supposed to believe that she's not your lover?"

His face clouded over again. "My dear, she goes everywhere by herself. It is one of the great vexations of my life that she can afford to follow me wherever I go."

"Then you're not engaged to her?"

"What! No, of course not. Did she tell you that? God, I'll throttle her," he swore. But then his tone became urgent again. "Listen to me. Sheilah and I had a fling once, it's true, but it was over long before I met you. She's neurotic, though, and simply will not let it rest. I think today may have done the trick, however."

"What do you mean?" she asked, puzzled.

James grinned wickedly. "When I realized that you had stalked off, I was furious. I blamed Sheilah—for which I see I was correct. We exchanged some rather unpleasant words and I pushed her into the harbor."

"James, you didn't!"

"I did," he affirmed solemnly, "and you've never heard such enthusiastic applause. The crew is even more sick of her than I am. So be warned: this is what happens to women who thwart me!"

A grin was working its way onto her face, but she wasn't yet ready to give in. "And what about Ms. Faulkner?"

"Jackie? What about her?"

"That night at your house. She said she was delivering papers from the office, but it was late and the way she was dressed—"

"Stop right there! So, you were listening from upstairs, were you? Well, Miss Snoop, she was indeed bringing me some rather important contracts that had just been flown in from California. Believe me, I had to do a great deal to make *that* up to her."

"Yes, I'm sure you rewarded her admirably." Nicole's eyes flashed dangerously.

"Why, you little . . . ! Listen to me. She was dressed as

184

she was because she was celebrating her anniversary with her husband that night, and—"

"Her *husband*?"

"Yes, she's married to my top salesman."

"But—but, she doesn't wear a wedding ring," she stammered.

"No," he admitted, "though I really don't know why. I never thought to ask. Perhaps she thinks it's unchic—she's terribly fashion conscious."

Now Nicole was laughing, a weak, joyous laugh of utter relief. She *had* been a fool! How could she have trusted him so little—or was it herself that she had distrusted? She could have known these things if she had only opened herself to him.

"Oh, I love you!" she whispered, throwing her arms around his neck. As he caught her his mouth found hers and for a long while they were lost in a storm of purely physical sensation.

It was very nearly dark when their passion finally lulled. There was only the faintest deep blue glow on the western horizon, and the bright moon was peeking on the opposite side of the sky.

As he led her slowly down the beach, waves broke around their bare feet in a green phosphorescent wash. She leaned against him, her arms wrapped around his hard torso, her head on his shoulder. His arm circled her protectively. He used it to pull her to him to be kissed every few yards.

"James," she complained weakly, putting her fingers lightly over his lips. "Won't they be wondering where we are?"

"Mmmm . . . I think they'll know," he muttered, planting a line of tantalizing kisses down the sensitive skin of her throat.

She groaned with pleasure and gave herself up to his demands.

Later, he asked, "You won't mind having your honeymoon here, will you? I don't think I can wait any longer, even though I know of at least two gentlemen back in Mannihasset who would love to give you away."

"H-honeymoon?"

"You silly goose. What did you think?" he scolded her gently. "That I merely wanted to add you to my string of conquests? You're much too special for that. Besides, I couldn't have won the race without you."

"But anyone could have done what I did," she protested.

"True. But not for just anyone would I have carried this all the way for good luck."

He reached into his pocket and, taking her left hand, slipped a ring on her finger. A tiny diamond sparkled in the moonlight.

Nicole caught her breath. "Oh, I—I—"

"Don't search for words, my love. Just say that, unlike some women, you'll never take it off. Say that you'll marry me."

"Yes!" she breathed.

It was the last coherent word she spoke for some time afterward.

A love forged by destiny—
A passion born of flame

FLAMES OF DESIRE

by Vanessa Royall

Selena MacPherson, a proud princess of ancient
Scotland, had never met a man who did not desire
her. From the moment she met Royce Campbell at
an Edinburgh ball, Selena knew the burning
ecstasy that was to seal her fate through all eternity.
She sought him on the high seas, in India, and
finally in a young America raging in the
birth-throes of freedom, where destiny was bound
to fulfill its promise. . . .

A DELL BOOK $2.95